SONS OF THUNDER

SONS OF THUNDER

Dave Hopwood

Authentic

MILTON KEYNES ● COLORADO SPRINGS ● HYDERABAD

14 13 12 11 10 09 08   8 7 6 5 4 3 2 1

First published 2008 by Authentic Media
9 Holdom Avenue, Bletchley, Milton Keynes, MK1 1QR, UK
1820 Jet Stream Drive, Colorado Springs, CO 80921, USA
OM Authentic Media, Medchal Road, Jeedimetla Village,
Secunderabad 500 055, A.P., India
www.authenticmedia.co.uk

Authentic Media is a division of IBS-STL U.K., limited by guarantee, with
its Registered Office at Kingstown Broadway, Carlisle, Cumbria CA3 0HA.
Registered in England & Wales No. 1216232. Registered charity 270162.

British Library Cataloguing in Publication Data
A catalogue record for this book is available from the British Library

ISBN-13: 978-1-85078-784-6

Cover Design by David Smart
Print Management by Adare
Printed in Great Britain by J.H. Haynes & Co., Sparkford

For Ken Wylie, Simeon Wood, Andy Page,
Tim Perry, Chris Hutchison, Chris Whitfield,
Kevin Huggett, Richard Haig, Paul Hobbs,
Pete Dudley, Peter Gunstone, Andy Hunter,
Alan Calaminusm and Stefan Brooks:

All those *sons* who, over the years, have kept me
off the straight and narrow.

Contents

He who saves one life . . . saves an entire universe.
The Talmud, Sanhedrin 4:5

Read it if you must

If you want to know what life is like for someone else, walk a mile in their shoes. If nothing else, you're then a mile away from them and you have their shoes.

A reporter once wanted to know what it was like to face the death penalty, so he chose to spend time on death row. He then intended to write about the experience so everyone could grasp something of it. When his time was up, the guards came to release him. Except they didn't release him. They marched him down the corridor and strapped him into the electric chair. Just another dead man walking. The reporter protested and wrestled and swore his innocence. Still they went on preparing to execute him. No one would listen.

The shock alone nearly killed him.

They wanted him to know what it was really like to face death and come out the other side.

Not just to pretend.

If I'm in paradise or prison, and I may end up in both on the same day, then what I need most is someone who can feel at home in either environment. Someone who understands both places. Someone who's been there ahead of me, who can sit with me in the squalor and laugh amongst the luxuries. The ultimate hero, I suppose.

Is it naïve to imagine that someone like that exists? That the ultimate hero is really out there? That there actually is someone who deserves my respect and allegiance? Seems daft – yet you have to wonder where the hankering for something more comes from. Why do we go looking for heroes? Why are we hungry for more stuff in our lives? New experiences . . . new gadgets . . . new toys . . . new supermen and celebrities? Could it possibly be a sign of a hankering for someone divine?

Certainly most people down the ages have been reaching for someone bigger, someone outside of themselves, someone larger than life itself. Secularism is surely a relatively new concept. Stumble upon most ancient civilisations, visit the most remote islands in the world and you'll find they have a place in their lives for deity.

If experience matters then, for me, one man's experience matters more than others. Forgive me for being dogmatic but I believe it more than anything else. (Though I can doubt it fiercely at 4 a.m. in the morning).

What you have here is not his story. But it is similar. A man who was, in his own words, 'the man' – all man – totally human. A man who lived life like you and I never have. We are just a shadow of this human being. This mysterious, powerful, vulnerable, witty, dangerous bloke.

No novel can sum him up, no book can even begin. So this is just a fragment of a portrait of 'the man'.

Thanks for buying this, borrowing it, or just picking it up in someone else's house. However you got it, and however much you read, I hope you find it's a thumping good book that leaves you entertained, encouraged and disturbed.

Dave Hopwood

The Bit before the First Bit

Eighteen years back

There were two boys sitting on the kerb. One said to the other 'Life sucks.'
The other said, 'Let's change it then.'
The rest is history.

A week later they are sitting in the same spot at the same time. But one of them is now in deep trouble.
'Why'd you run off in London today?'
'I didn't run off in London.'
'Not what I heard.'
Across the street, four younger boys kick a ball about. Behind them, terraced windows shine blue with the glow of early evening television.
'The word is the police were looking for you.'
'They found me.'
'So d'you get arrested then?'
The four boys stop kicking the ball and stare over. One of them yells.
'You got a police record?'
'Course not. I just bumped into a load of people who talk a lot.'
'Where?'

'Sounds boring.'

'What d'you do with them?'

The questions rain down on them like a spray of gravel on a tin roof.

'I talked a lot and then the police came.'

'What d'you talk about?'

'Stuff.'

'Football?'

'No, stuff.'

'Meet anyone famous?'

'Yea, any footballers?'

'Dunno. There were some people off the telly.'

'Did you get handcuffed? With a bag on your head?'

'No, I got grounded. By my dad.'

The other boys have had enough now, they go back to their kicking and shirt pulling.

Two boys sit by the kerb and one says to the other, 'How you gonna change the world if you're grounded?'

'I'll wait till I'm not grounded. I'm in no rush.'

'I am. I know, we'll make a blood pact. I'll start changing everything and you can finish it.'

'What's a blood pact?'

'Something they do in cowboy movies. It means you can't change it.'

'Whose blood do we use?'

'Yours.'

'Oh, thanks!'

'Your blood's cleverer than mine.'

'What?'

'My blood couldn't go to the big city and talk to lots of famous people.'

'Bet it could. Bet it will one day.'

'Shut up and give us your blood.'

'How?'

'Drag your wrist on the ground till it bleeds.'
One of the boys scrapes his wrist on the pavement and winces as the red liquid oozes from his torn flesh. The two of them rub the heels of their hands together. The pact is sealed.
The rest is detail. The rest really is history.

First Bit

One toe at a time

My name is Tom. I'm thirty-two. I grew up on the south-west coast of England, in a small beach town in Cornwall. A place of summer surf and wild winter storms.

What I'm about to tell you is based on real events and took place more than ten years ago.

I guess you can decide for yourself which bits to believe.

As far as I'm concerned, I have to get this out as quickly as possible. I'm about to die because of what happened.

I'm not going to waste time telling you about my parents, or my schooling, or my student days. All you need to know is I didn't do well. I left home at eighteen in a blaze of glory and returned a year later with nothing but a nervous breakdown and a drink problem.

I got over the breakdown, but the drinking hung around. That's how I met the lads. I was mooching in the corner of the Limping Greyhound one early summer night, nursing my pint and musing on what I might have done with my miserable life. I'd spent the last however many years watching porn and drinking away my

unemployment benefit. I'd even managed to con the
government into handing me some business start-up
funds. A mate helped me. I was gonna set up my own
woodcarving business with the cash. I drank it all
instead.

I say 'mate', but I didn't really have any mates. This
guy lived round the corner and his old man sometimes
worked with my old man. That's as far as it went really.
He was just good at filling in forms.

I was just a loser, drowning in my own little ocean of
Guinness. Funny thing was, there was a certain morbid
pleasure to it all – a certain kind of relief in not having to
try any more. I'd quite clearly failed and everyone could
see it and smell it. Curling up in a corner and commit-
ting slow suicide was no big deal really. What was so
wrong with admitting defeat, stepping out of the race
and letting everyone else get on with their flimsy
attempts at making life work?

I was content to stagger home from non-work and flip
on Sky Scandinavian Three. It made sense – there was a
certain chaotic rhythm to it all. Beer was softly battering
my body, porn quietly corroding my mind. Self-destruc-
tion felt dangerous and exciting. A bit like a cannibal on
his own desert island, surviving by eating himself, one
toe at a time.

Counterfeit Clash

The lads were huddled round a video game. There was
a lot of shouting about scores and virtual bad guys.

When I was a kid, we didn't have violent computer
games. Those were happier times. We just played games
like Best Man Dead, i.e. who could pretend to die in the
most barbaric and horrific fashion. Skewered on a meat

hook, burnt alive by flame-thrower, melting in an acid bath, that sort of thing. The land of make-believe.

Games were more educational, too. I had a chemistry set so that I could discover the wonders of the elemental table and chemical reactions. It came in handy for melting Airfix soldiers in the burner and torturing them in vials of boiling water.

As I stumbled to the bar and overheard the killing cries from the video crowd I remembered lighting matches and flinging them at my very best friend. Ah. Happy days.

I noticed that the guy who'd helped me with the business start-up stuff was with them. He was just like the others – shaved head, earring and tattoos – they all looked alike to me. Thin as rakes, ripped drainpipe jeans and boots like black cabs. I think he was a bit older than the others, but not much. Only Jack and Jimmy stood out from the crowd, with their intimidating good looks, their groomed, bleached surfer hair, and their all-year tans. My mate spotted me and gave me a quick nod. I nodded back and tried not to look drunk. It was no mean achievement.

'How's the business going?' he called.

He turned away from the crowd and took a step towards me.

'Oh! You know . . .' I bluffed, 'ups and downs. Good days, bad days.'

He nodded again and went back to watching the game. Oddly, something inside of me wanted to yell out an apology. Tell him I'd deposited the money straight down the toilet.

But I didn't. I just went to the bar and spent some more.

'Want to come out and see the Counterfeit Clash?'

'What?'

Five shaved heads and two bleached ones looked over at me as I got my drink.

'We got tickets.'

'They're like the Clash.'

'But they're not really them.'

'So it's fake.'

'Counterfeit.'

They all kind of contributed to the explanation, but it happened so fast I couldn't keep up with who said what.

Bullet words coming at me across the blurry gap between me and them.

'I don't know, I . . .'

Truth was I'd had a skinful and going anywhere at that moment required a lot of concentration. Plus, I never went anywhere with anyone back then. No one wanted me around. I glanced at Jimmy and Jack. They certainly didn't look like they wanted me around. It was the others, the grinning skinheads, who'd invited me.

'Come on, we have to go now if we're gonna go.'

This last remark was directed at no one in particular. They all supped up, grabbed jackets and headed for the door. One of them glanced back. It was him again, my business start-up mate, Josh his name was.

'Well, coming or not?' he said.

I wanted to tell him not – but instead I found myself chucking two-thirds of a pint down my throat and following them.

We walked through the warm night towards the town hall. Whoever the Counterfeit Clash were, they didn't play Hammersmith Palais.

Burgers

The place was jammed with bodies; most of them male, most of them sporting shaved heads. I tried to ruffle my hair to make it appear spiked, but you can't do a lot with a forest of wire curls.

A warm-up band was playing on a stage too small for them. I counted fifteen up there, including two drummers and three saxophone players. The rest carried guitars and did a variety of things with them. The noise was deafening.

Jimmy sniffed the air and yelled, 'Burgers!'

'I'll get 'em!' Josh yelled and he tugged my arm and took me along.

We queued for a long time while the band played on. By the time we got there, the news was bad. An old guy with an eye-patch and broken teeth was serving; he shook his head when we ordered eight burgers with beer.

'Only got two burgers and some Coke left,' he shouted, and he had to say it twice for us to hear.

'There'll be trouble,' I said.

We took what he'd got and fought our way back through the sweating bodies. The guys weren't where we'd left them. They were nowhere to be seen.

We dumped the food and drink and I elected to guard the supply while Josh went on the hunt.

I hadn't stood there long when a fat hand reached over and grabbed one of the polystyrene boxes.

'Hey! Leave that!'

I said it before I looked up at him. Had I looked first I probably would have offered him everything on the table, wrapped in the shirt off my back. A biker in black loomed over me, along with two other men-mountains in hellfire red. Now I'm not short, but these guys were like gladiators. Albeit fat gladiators with filthy black hair and beards like oily rags.

'You wanna say that again?' the biker grabbed my shirt and hoiked me into his chest. He smelt of cigarettes and petrol.

'Not really,' I muttered, but I doubt he heard my whimper.

He nodded to the others and they scooped up the food.

'We ain't gonna leave you empty-handed, though,' he said and the guys in red dumped a pile of empty burger cartons on the table.

Before I knew it he'd slapped me round the head twice and sauntered off with the other two, taking our food and Coke with them.

There seemed little reason to stay guarding the table now. In fact, I couldn't think of a reason to stay at all, so I put my head down and made for the door. I barged through, staring hard at the floor, trying to cut a path through the bodies, and this was the reason I walked smack into the whole crowd of guys coming the other way.

'Oh, it's you . . .' It was them, Josh and his buddies. 'Look guys, I gotta go . . .'

'Show us the food, man,' shouted Jimmy and he steered me back to face the way I'd come.

I led them miserably back to the stack of empty cartons. They crowded round the pile and frowned.

'A couple of big hairy guys mugged me,' I said.

A good forty-five seconds of head-slapping and jibing followed. Jimmy and Jack grabbed me by the collar and ordered me to take them to the less-than-dandy highwaymen.

It wasn't hard to find the bad guys and, when the others had seen, they nodded and shrugged.

'It was only a couple of burgers,' they said and we crept into the shadows.

On the way we were intercepted by one of our guys.

This guy stood out from the others, head and shoulders above the crowd. I'd not noticed him before but there was something about him. I guess you'd say he was a natural leader. Broad-shouldered, confident, looked like he knew what was coming next.

'Come here,' he said, his voice an effortless rumble.

He took us over to the table where we'd left the empty food cartons.

It was piled high with burgers and bottles of Heineken.

'What the . . .?'

'But there was only empties here . . .'

'I thought you said there weren't any more burgers left?' Jack said, looking at Josh and me.

I turned to the big guy.

'Where did these come from?' I asked.

The big guy grinned and shrugged.

'Tuck in,' he said.

And so we did.

Swimming with sharks

After the gig we made our way down to the beach and clambered over the rocks and around the coast. The water was raging, black and white breakers smashing over our feet as we sat staring into the dark.

Jack and Jimmy had met up with two girls in the Clash gig, Sal and Miz. Pretty stunning, both of them. Sal, tall and confident, with tumbling wild hair and a constant smile; Miz, shorter and louder, her red hair spiked fiercely and a million earrings jangling around her neck. The guys had brought them along and I guessed they felt their luck was in.

It was odd hanging around with these people I barely knew. I was older than all of them and would never have put myself on a rock on a dark night with them. But for a few moments I could pretend I belonged, wasn't just a miserable loner sat in the Greyhound mumbling into his pint. For a while there, it felt almost good.

We'd been sitting for a while, flinging rocks and shells into the foam, and bragging about stuff when there was a yelp from the girls.

A couple of the guys had grabbed Miz and hoisted her off her feet. It was Jimmy and Jack and they were headed for the edge of the rocks. Sal threw a few wild punches and tried to pull them back, but no one else was trying to stop them.

Miz screamed as they grabbed her arms and legs and hung her over the edge. She kicked and tore a foot free, but Jack grabbed it again.

'Hope you can swim,' cautioned Jack as they swung her once, twice, three times towards the wild sea below.

She shouted something like, 'Don't do it!'

And no one really thought they would.

But the blond guys weren't listening, they were just clocking each other and grinning, their white teeth glinting in the dark, willing each other on. They swung her up and back one more time. She seemed to hover in the air for a second.

Then there was a yelp and a cry as they let go and the body went crashing into the water.

'What did she say just then?' shouted Jimmy, his big hand pushing back the blond streaks from his eyes.

'Dunno.'

'She said, she can't swim!' said Sal.

'What?'

'Was she joking?'

Sal shook her head fiercely and shoved Jack. 'Don't be stupid. Do something!'

A glimmer of a white face appeared in the dark sea. The girl's arms were flailing and she was screaming and shrieking at us.

For some reason no one moved. Her face disappeared into the water. We looked at one another but still no one did anything. She appeared again, her arms beating the water, but making no attempts to swim back to us. She slipped under and reappeared, yelled then disappeared. We watched but she didn't resurface.

'She really can't swim,' screamed Sal, pushing me and Jack closer to the edge. 'Ah, you're hopeless! If you aren't going in then I . . .'

Suddenly I felt a shove from behind and I almost fell onto Jack as a body pushed past me. It was the big guy, the natural leader. He powered through and dived into the water. At the same moment the girl reappeared. She was thrashing about like a dying shark in there, and the waves were crashing into each other like cars in a bad traffic accident, but somehow he got to her straight away, cupped an arm round her neck and towed her back towards the shore. He lifted her up and placed her on the rock in one move.

'Wow! Cool, man!'

There was much appreciation and backslapping as the big guy hauled himself from the black water, but as he straightened up, his face looked like a disfigured mask.

'Don't ever do anything like that again,' he said, and everyone shut up straight away. He stared at Jack and Jimmy.

'Stay out of my way, ya blond bimbos.'

Jimmy's fist recoiled like a snake preparing for the strike, but Jack grabbed his hand and pulled it down.

'Easy,' Jack muttered, 'he ain't worth it.'

Jimmy cleared his throat and spat on the rock between the big man's feet. The big guy glanced down and shook his head.

'Loser,' he muttered and he slammed a massive hand into Jimmy's chest and pushed his way through the crowd of us. We watched him go, and then fell on the rocks beside Miz.

She was shocked and soaked, and lashed out at Jack and Jimmy with a hail of exhausted wild slaps. Jimmy threw a few slaps back but Jack just grinned at her.

I turned and stared at the big man. He was making his way back towards the land.

'Who is that guy?' I asked as we started back over the rocks.

But no one said anything. No one was listening to me.

94,608,000 seconds

And then I didn't see them again for three years. A few of the guys went to university and disappeared from the local scene, the others got jobs and vanished off my radar.

I didn't know it was going to be three years. To me, it was just endless time. Days going nowhere, nights I couldn't remember. But one man's wasteland is another man's building site.

Who'd have thought that so many days could have made so much difference? It was only 94,608,000 seconds. But every tick of the clock was bringing it closer. Every time I fell into bed, every time I fell out, every time I mooched into the Greyhound and wished away another three hours, every time I switched on *Top Gear* or sat through another repeat of *Men Behaving Badly*, every time I ate another vindaloo and downed another ocean of Guinness. Tick, tick, tick.

Every time I glanced drunkenly at those digital figures and registered the useless passing of another dead day, it wasn't just another 86,400 seconds . . . all the while something was happening. All the while the future was brewing. Way off, over the horizon of my life . . . something was coming. Something I couldn't conceive. It was getting closer with every second, and it was coming right round the corner at me.

Second Bit

Small and shabby

I couldn't believe it when I next saw my mate from round the corner, Josh, the one who'd helped me with the business start-up. The boy next door was now the man about town. He'd bulked up, grown his hair and put on trendy clothes. His face lit up as soon as he saw me.

'Tom! Hey! It's me. How's it going?'

Terrible. Worse than ever. Thought about suicide all last week.

'Oh, fine. You've changed a bit.'

'Yea, been working with my old man, doing painting and decorating. Hey, come with me, I want you to meet someone.'

'Now?'

'Yea, he's just in the other bar.'

We were in the Greyhound and I was on my third pint and suddenly found myself hanging around with a whole group of unrecognisables. It turned out they were just the rest of the guys, three years later. They'd had lives, moved on. I hadn't. A few of the lads had just got back from uni and they were having some kind of reunion.

Two of the guys were chatting together at the bar. We went over, though I wasn't in the mood for introductions. I'd had too much to drink as usual and I felt small and shabby next to these two. Before we could say much, another voice bellowed at us across the pub. I didn't recall the voice but I knew the face. And the black leathers. And the wild matted hair. It was the nasty biker. The one who stole our burgers and Coke. He'd come back for more. He made his way over, this time accompanied by a bunch of people who looked nothing like him, though they clearly hung on his every word. The biker thrust a fat finger at us.

'You wanna watch this guy,' he said, jabbing at us, 'big things are gonna follow in his wake.'

I looked around but he jabbed so quickly I couldn't work out who he was talking about.

He was speaking to his groupies, all a lot younger and tidier than he was.

'This guy is gonna change the world,' he went on. 'Trust me. I know what I'm talking about.'

I don't know if a hush came over the bar after he'd said this, or if it was just my imagination. Either way, his comment hung in the air for a few seconds afterwards. It was clear to me that this guy had spent the last three years in cloud cuckoo land. He was a joke – so why was I the only one grinning?

The biker nodded meaningfully at us and gave me a final wink before turning away. His groupies went with him, already debating the awesome wisdom of his outburst. One of his mates hung around though and stayed with us. His name was Andy, and I'd seen him in the Greyhound a few times before.

'What was that all about?' I muttered to him.

'You'll find out,' Andy said. 'Don't judge a biker by his leathers.'

We returned to the introductions. It turned out the big guy next to me was Si, the natural-born leader who'd rescued Miz three years ago. He'd filled out even more, muscled up, and added designer stubble to his good looks.

The guy with him was Jude – older than the rest, smoother, leaner and dressed in expensive gear. Not the Limping Greyhound type at all. I'd never seen him before.

They both muttered and nodded and gave me the time of day, but I still felt small and shabby.

Clay disc carnage

And I guess it's true to say that after that my life was never the same again. Oh, I still felt like suicide when I woke up each morning, and I still taped the porn channels at night. But my visits to the Greyhound were not only about swimming in the Guinness. Now I was on the lookout for big Si, and cool Jude, and gorgeous Sal, and Andy.

I soon discovered Andy was big Si's brother. He didn't look it: if Si was the mountain, Andy was the molehill. He was a friendly guy though, and I started to get to know him; he didn't have the kind of aura that kept me away from big Si. Andy always gave me a smile and bought me a pint. He was the nicest guy I'd ever met. Apart from Josh.

'Where is Josh these days?' I asked Andy one day. 'I never see him now. It's like he's disappeared.'

Andy shrugged. 'He said he had to go away for a few days. Probably visiting his old dear.'

'But his old dear lives round the corner from me,' I said. 'He wouldn't go away to see her.'

'Oh, he's probably job hunting,' Andy said. 'Tom, you ever been shooting?'

'What?'

'You ever been shooting? Nat's got a couple of shotguns and all the gear for shooting clay. The Old Mariner's got acres of empty woodland behind it. Come and hang out with us.'

'Now?' I asked.

'No, you doghead,' said Andy, 'not now. Tomorrow.'

'I'm busy.' I said. 'What did he say?'

'Who?'

'Josh. What did he say about where he was going?'

'Mars. He said he was going to Mars, all right? Now you coming shooting or not? Ten o'clock tomorrow. I'll meet you on the seafront by the old pier. If you're not there, me and Nat'll come looking.'

I didn't really know Nat, just seen him hanging around with the others. He was a weedy guy with no hair and dull grey eyes who played the slot machines in the Greyhound. He'd been around for the past three years but we never spoke or bought each other a drink. I just saw him across a crowded bar sometimes. Now suddenly we were bosom buddies, and I was going to handle firearms with him. And that's how the whole shooting match started. Once a week we'd meet up, Nat would bring his guns and we'd slip through a break in the fence of the derelict Old Mariner hotel. The place had lain empty for two years and no one cared what went on in the overgrown acreage at the back. Wild grass gave way to rampant woodland and in the heart of the trees there was a massive clearing, full of old litter and used condoms. It was a potholed mess but it was also ideal for a spot of clay pigeon shooting. There were old tree stumps for sitting on. Judging by the number of spent shotgun shells lying around, we weren't the only ones to drop by for a spot of clay disc carnage.

I started to enjoy those mornings with Andy, Nat and the guns, though Nat talked an awful lot of rubbish. Spring was kicking in and the weather was perking up. It wasn't so much the shooting, I just loved sitting around twisting bits of twigs, supping Coke and chatting about what we'd do if we had loads of money. Nat was dead serious about the shooting, but I figured I'd never get that serious about anything.

Then Josh came back.

Coke adds life

I don't know how long he'd been away. I kind of lost track of time. Maybe a week, maybe four, maybe more. It just seemed as if he wasn't around for a while, and then he reappeared. He looked leaner, there were circles under his eyes and his cheeks were hollow.

And for some reason the first place he came to was our clearing in the grounds of the Old Mariner. I was on my own, loading up Nat's shotgun, when I noticed a lone figure standing in the shadows.

'Hi, Tom.'

'Josh, where you been?'

'Away.'

'I know that,' I said, 'I took up shooting. Look.'

I offered him the gun.

'I can see,' he said.

'Are you OK?' I asked him. 'You look . . . hungry.'

He staggered and put his hand out to grab the tree nearest to him. It was an old beech tree, and he gripped at the bark, but his hand slipped and he staggered and fell against it.

'Josh, what's going on . . .?'

'I've had a difficult time . . .' he slurred his words as he spoke.

He slipped down to a crouch and slumped against the trunk. He rested his head against the bark and shut his eyes.

'I've been awake for a long time,' he muttered.

Nat and Andy reappeared then; they'd been away buying Coke and doughnuts.

Andy dropped his bag when he spotted Josh on his knees and came running over.

'Josh, you look a mess,' Andy said. 'Come on, let's get you something to eat . . .'

'Worst case scenario . . .' Nat muttered. He had this annoying thing he always said, when it meant nothing really. 'Worst case scenario . . . worst case scenario . . .' He said it all the time, and he repeated it now as he just stood there, shaking his head.

Andy helped Josh into the clearing and I just watched, wishing I'd had the initiative to help him up myself. Andy sat Josh on a tree trunk and fed him Coke and doughnuts. Josh ate slowly and carefully, as if he'd not done it for a while. Nat took up a gun and started cleaning it.

'Look at the state of this, man. Worst case scenario. Worst case. You never clean it, dude, after you've used it. Total worst case. You should clean these things, they're like children, man, total worst case . . .' And he went on muttering like that for a while. He always muttered at length. We just ignored most of it.

'I don't know how to clean 'em,' I snapped. 'Josh, what's going on?'

Josh smiled weakly. 'I'm fine,' he said. 'I got lots to tell you, but I can't do it now.'

'You look like you've been in a war zone, dude, like you've been totalled, man!' Nat said.

Josh laughed. 'You'd better believe it,' he said, 'Nat, you're a man of distinction and integrity . . .' and with that he lurched forward onto his stomach and passed out.

We carried him to the car, laid him on the back seat and drove him back to my flat. I say a flat – it was one room up some stairs on a first floor that tripled for a kitchen, bedroom and lounge with a yard down the fire escape at the back. It was my uncle's bachelor pad (and it looked like it) but he long gave up that kind of life and tolerated me squatting there. We took Josh inside, laid him out on my bed for a while and waited.

The strange thing was, when he woke up again, he was as right as rain. His energy was back and the rings under his eyes had gone; I know Coke adds life, but it had to be more than that.

Bad Lassie

Besides his leathers and his oily hair, Biker John had a bull neck and a dog to match. We found 'em both one day standing out on the beach – and everyone else had found 'em, too. Not sure how long he'd been around there but he was acting weird, going on about the death of the planet. It was like a joke but no one was laughing. Round here, people have got spooked about the planet anyway lately and this guy seemed to be cashing in.

'Stop polluting the place with your lifestyle,' he was yelling. 'The place is doomed if you keep living this way. Change your minds and change your life.'

People were lapping it up, dousing themselves in sea water as some kind of pact to be better stewards or something. I didn't get it. His dog kept getting frisky and trying to make babies with other people's legs. It was like another planet. People standing around shivering in the sea, Biker John berating them for the size of their carbon footprints, while Bad Lassie got up close and personal with their ankles.

When Biker John saw me standing there with Josh he jabbed a fat finger at us and thundered, 'I told you he was coming. I'm just the warm-up act. I told you before. I'm nearly done now. But he's just getting started. When I last saw that guy he was heading for the badlands. Well, he's back, and you'd better watch out because the planet's about to rattle on its axis. He'll send it spinning the opposite way, and anyone not wearing a safety harness will be flung into oblivion.'

What the heck was he on about?

Not normal at all

About a week later, the big biker guy got arrested. Can't say I was surprised really. The story on the street was possession of drugs and disturbing the peace. But everyone knew he never touched drugs. Disturbing the peace, maybe. He'd been hanging around on the wrong street corners, yelling about corruption in local council. He seemed to have picked up some tasty morsels about the mayor and the local MP. I didn't take too much notice but I know that it involved rent boys and misuse of government funds. Anyway, surprise, surprise, the big man got picked up by the Bill and given free accommodation for a while.

The day the news broke in the headlines, Josh burst into the Greyhound at lunchtime, all bright-eyed and bushy-tailed.

'All right,' he said, 'I need some help. It's time to get things going.'

Josh just had not been the same guy since that day in the clearing. Every time I saw him he seemed a little more confident.

'We need to put some wheels on this machine,' he said, as he hoiked me out of the pub and took me down to Si's garage.

I thought he meant literally for a while, but I knew he had no motor and couldn't drive. And when he got to the garage, he spent half an hour chatting to Si and Andy. For the first time, Si no longer had the aura round him. He was angry about some Merc he was trying to fix. Swearing and cussing about being up half the night and getting nowhere.

As I helped myself to a Coke from his machine I watched Josh in the cracked mirror on the wall. He leant over the open bonnet, stuck his head deep inside for a minute, then reappeared covered in engine oil.

'Try it now,' he said.

Si looked at him and laughed.

'Josh, you know nothing about cars. I shouldn't let you within ten paces of this thing.'

'Try the engine.'

I sensed the balance of power shifting. Till now everyone had looked to Si. This 'Try the engine' stuff from Josh was not normal. Not normal at all.

Si was mad. You could see it in his eyes. He was ready to kill something. I stood watching with my Coke unopened. Andy hovered in the background, I guess trying to work out how to be friendly about the worsening situation.

'I'll do it!' Andy suddenly volunteered as Josh and Si stared each other out.

Si didn't bother saying anything to his little brother. He didn't have to. His silence put the boy in his place. Si walked stiffly round to the driver's door, threw it open and sat inside. He was still staring stone-faced at Josh as he jerked the key round in the ignition.

There was an angry roar and the engine settled into a steady purr. Si just sat and stared at Josh for the longest time.

Things were changing.

Sedition and flatulence

I love the summer. Especially the first time you feel the heat on your face. You don't know the moment's coming until it hits you from nowhere, and then you realise – you haven't felt the force of that summer sun since last year. It ignites your bones and reminds you of when you were a kid, when summer holidays went on forever, and the start of them was always filled with the smell of cut grass and the promise of endless days of freedom and possibilities.

This day I felt that heat for the first time. Summer was coming. I'd spent so many recent summers hiding in the Greyhound, it felt good and strange to be outside, sitting in the clearing watching Nat clean his shotguns.

Andy was there, and Si too. It was a week after the garage incident. When the warmth washed over me I remembered childhood days and it felt again as if promise was in the air. Maybe this summer would be different to the last twenty-one.

We were discussing the incident with the Merc. Si had been withdrawn and brooding ever since. Not that I knew him well at all; Si was someone I never got close too. Too big, too powerful. He sat there on a rock smoking, and strumming his old battered guitar. He was a Bruce Cockburn fan and was growling a song about some son of a bitch dying.

'Hey dudes, did you hear about Biker John? Worst case scenario,' Nat said. 'Worst case. Totally.'

'What d'you mean?' I asked.

'The big biker dude got arrested.'

'Yea, I know. But they'll have to let him go soon,' I said.

'They won't,' said Nat. 'They've totalled him, shipped him off to London. Worst case. Thrown the book at him.'

'What?' I couldn't believe it.

'Yea, they're charging him with sedition, treason, drug possession, a whole load of things.'

'Is treason still a crime?' said Andy, tossing a bottle in the air and cracking it with a stone.

'Course it is,' said Si, 'they just can't hang you for it.'

He dumped his guitar in the sand and started laying cards on a tree stump for another game of solitaire. The guy seemed to play a lot of solitaire.

'Oh, it's all trumped up,' said Andy. 'They're scared – he knows too much and he ain't afraid to say it out loud. The papers reckon he was mixed up with suicide bombers and the like.'

'Yea, dude, right,' said Nat. 'And Elvis ain't dead and Yoda's not a puppet. Chuck us that cloth, Andy.'

'He was weird though,' I said. 'I mean, what happened to him? He went from burger-stealing nutter to manic street preacher overnight.'

'Not overnight, mate,' said Andy. 'It had been coming for a while.'

'I tell you one crime they could have charged him with,' said Nat. 'Indecent flatulence in a public place. Man, that guy could break wind for England. Worst case scenario. No debate, could have taken out the White House with one of them stooges.'

'He was on some weird diet, cockroaches and dead leaves or something. Played havoc with his guts.'

Nat laughed and nodded like a toy dog in the back window of a car. 'Played havoc with mine too,' he said.

'How did Biker John know all that stuff?' I said.

'I dunno,' said Nat. 'Ask Josh. He knows.'

'Josh?'

'Yea, he's his cousin, dude.'

'I didn't know that.'

'There's plenty you don't know, man, plenty. Worst case when it comes to knowing stuff, you are.'

There were often moments like that. Just when I thought I was part of things, Nat would toss me that kind of hand-grenade. He had this mean streak, proba-bly cause he felt on the edge too. Nat was a traffic war-den – and we all know what everyone thinks of them. He spent his days dealing u-o-me tickets and dodging punches. There were times when listening to him drivel on made me want to punch his lights out.

Jack and Jimmy ran a surf shop, hiring boards and sell-ing wetsuits and all the trendy gear. They were the embodiment of cool. They fell out of bed in the morning with their hair in a designer mess and lived immaculate lives full of women and sport. They didn't know how to lose. Unlike Si and Andy, who ran their old man's garage and had lives full of chaos and loans. They barely made ends meet – and Si was often in a black mood about the struggle to get by, but not Andy; the two brothers were like chalk and cheese.

Jude came and went when he felt like it, never seemed to do that much work-wise. He knew a lot of people and spent his time talking on corners. He struck deals in the darkest pubs and always had money. Yet, out of all of us he seemed to be the one who had a handle on Josh. And Josh – well, Josh couldn't seem to decide what to do. His old man wanted him to take over the family decorating business, but Josh didn't seem that keen. Truth was,

Josh's family wanted him to do a lot of things he didn't want to do. He had four brothers and three sisters and the moment things started to change they all thought he was bonkers. They started booking him appointments with NHS shrinks. He never kept 'em. It must have been a nightmare for him.

I sound like I know what I'm talking about, as if these guys were my bosom buddies. But the truth is I was still spending most of my days alone with my pint. Shooting with Nat and Andy was the highlight of my week, and some weeks even that didn't happen.

One big mother

Now, Si and Andy may have run their old man's garage, but Jack and Jimmy's surf shop, Breakers, was secretly run by their mother. No secret really; she was one hell of a scary mama. She ran the business like the Kray's mum – quietly in the background, an ever-present maternal shadow. She was a tiny woman, no more than five feet. But what she lacked in size she made up for in mental prowess. And mental was a good word for it. Nobody messed with her, nobody stood up to her. Not even big Si. In times gone by her old man, Jack and Jimmy's grandfather, had been a revolutionary in the Spanish Civil War. The whole family had rebel blood in its veins and it was still lurking there in Jack and Jimmy; they just took out their aggression on the sea. And the gambling.

Jack and Jimmy played poker. They loved it. They'd play into the wee small hours in a back room of the surf shop. Nat was in on it, though he assured us repeatedly he never had any money. Probably because of the poker. Other surf dudes were part of it too. Summer was the time of year when the syndicate really took off. More guys around to take part, more visitors to fleece. Jack and Jimmy lived for their poker.

Mama Kray wasn't part of that, though it's said she sometimes pitched up with a tray of malt whisky and slices of Battenberg.

I only know this from hearsay. I wasn't invited and never had the money or the inclination to join in. I just sat in the Greyhound and listened to the stories from a distance.

Breakers was perched right on the edge of the sand, ideally placed for the summer business. Jack and Jimmy had never had much time for Josh. Then he started winning at poker.

Josh first showed up out of the blue, during one big game, early that summer. Like me, he never played poker, or at least no one had ever seen him do it, but he sat in for a few nights, and won a few games. Jack and Jimmy started to take notice. Fifth night in, Josh won a massive stash. Hundreds of quid. At three in the morning, the others drifted off the worse for wear. Josh invited the brothers for an early morning stroll along the beach (they were twins actually – did I say? No matter, they were). They watched him stuff his pockets with the cash then followed him out into the dying night.

I only know what happened because Jack told me a couple of years later. While they walked, Josh told them he had a plan. That he had no intention of going into his old man's decorating business. He had lots of ideas in his head but wasn't ready to talk about them. What he needed was some guys who'd help him out. He said there'd be travelling, adventure, and plenty of the unknown.

I think it must have sounded a bit criminal to the twins, which is probably why they sat up and took notice. Either way, by the time the sun came up he'd won 'em over. Somehow, by telling them next to nothing, he'd persuaded them to come on board with his plan. Whatever that was. He clinched the deal by fishing in his pockets and pulling out his winnings.

'Have this lot back,' he said. 'I don't need it right now. Maybe one day, but not now.'

And with that, Josh turned and strolled off into the sunrise, leaving the surf dudes standing on the sand, dazed and bewildered.

I was hanging out with Andy the next day at the garage when Jack and Jimmy rolled up. They were in Jack's silver BMW – and pulled up looking like a couple of extras from *Miami Vice*.

Si came tanking out like a fire engine on Guy Fawkes Night.

'What d'you want? We're busy,' he snarled.

Jimmy curled his top lip and said, 'That's not what I heard.' He pushed open his door and Si had to step back to let him out.

'Shame to see a place like this go down the tubes,' said Jimmy.

'It ain't going down the tubes,' said Si, 'and, if you don't mind, we need this bit of ground that your brother's scrapheap is sitting on right now.'

Jimmy sneered and glanced around, there wasn't another car in sight.

'What for? Sunbathing?' he said.

Si placed his huge hand on Jimmy's chest. They were both big men but Si towered over Jimmy.

'If I were you I'd leave here while you can still walk.'

Si and Jimmy stared at one another.

Jack climbed from the driver's side.

'We just want to ask you something,' Jack said.

'What?' Si kept his eyes drilling into Jimmy's head as he spoke.

'We reckon Josh is hatching something, something big. Something that we might want to get into.'

'Yea,' said Jimmy, 'and we don't think you need to get into it too.'

Si laughed, a big bellow of a laugh that made Jimmy recoil.

'Since when did you two tell me how to run my life?'

Jack sat casually on the bonnet of the BMW. He nodded and ran a hand slowly through his blond hair.

'Look, it's obvious this business matters to you, you need to put some energy into it. It's a good investment. Why waste your time hanging around with the likes of Josh? Or,' and Jack almost visibly winced as he added, 'the likes of us. You don't need that. You got plenty of other things to do.'

Si stepped away from Jimmy.

'I get it,' he said. 'Josh wants you in his posse and you're scared of having to work with me.'

'Has he asked you, then?' Jack said.

Si threw a glance at his brother. 'He's asked us both,' he said.

'To do what?'

Si shrugged. 'To do whatever he asked you two to do.' He picked up a massive wrench and swung it menacingly. Jack sighed and nodded.

'Well, we'd better make sure we don't kill each other in the process. Just stay on the other side of the road and we'll be cool.'

'I'll stay wherever I want to stay.'

'We'll see about that,' said Jimmy.

Si gestured with the wrench but Jimmy didn't flinch, he just eased himself back into the passenger seat.

Jack and Jimmy drove away, Jimmy proffering a finger as they went.

Si went back to work.

'Why d'you guys hate each other?' I said as Andy and I watched them go.

'Cause they think they own the place. Always have. Playgroup, school, life. It's always been the same. They won't live and let live. It's been brewing for years. The problem for them is – whenever Si opens his mouth everyone looks to him, not them. I just hope Josh realises what he's taken on here.'

Third Bit

Keeping our heads down

When I met Josh the next week, he didn't mention his chat with Jack and Jimmy.

'What you doing Saturday?' he asked as he and I sat in the Greyhound supping Guinness.

I shrugged. Same as what I did every Saturday. Nothing.

'Wanna come to a wedding? My cousin's getting hitched.'

That reminded me, I wanted to ask him about another cousin of his.

'Two o'clock at the church for the do and then three o'clock at the Granada for a good time.'

I winced. I hadn't been to church in years.

'It's all right,' he said, 'it'll be fine. We'll slip in the back and keep our heads down.'

And it would have been fine if only we'd stuck to that plan.

We arrived late and there were a lot of people. So it was standing room only. It was a beautiful warm day, perfect for a wedding, and the inside of the little church was cool and full of the smell of flowers. We slipped down a side aisle and hid behind a pillar. I was surprised to see Jack and Jimmy there, and blow me, Si too. Had Josh invited them? Why?

Everything was kosher for a while, boring but kosher. Not having a seat proved to be an advantage as we didn't have to bother about all that stand up, sit down, kneel down malarkey. But then the preacher got up and the sermon started.

He was the local vicar, been around for years. I didn't know him but my old man had done some furnishing work on his house and they'd been on nodding terms ever since.

The old guy was having a bit of trouble reading the Bible bit before he started talking; the print was too small or his glasses were the wrong sort. That's when Josh stuck a finger in the air and volunteered to read it for him. There was a bit of commotion at first cause this was well unplanned, but then Josh's cousin, the bride, saw it was him and looked well chuffed that he'd volunteered. Josh gave her a big grin and stepped up to read.

'Many have dreamt of freedom. Of captives set free, wrongs put right, cruelty replaced with justice, abuse displaced by kindness. Martin Luther King dreamt. So did Ghandi. Mandela, Mother Teresa and Bono. They all dreamt and the dream goes on and with the living of their lives they give their dream to us. But today I'm here to tell you – this is more than a dream. The dream is giving birth to reality. You see, the God of hope is coming, and actually is already here, heavily disguised. In the cracks, in the shady corners, in the mess and the stains of everyday life. In the slums and the brothels, in the whispers of the humble and the screams of the wounded. He sits in dark prisons and ill-equipped hospitals, in the foodless kitchens and freezing homes. He's the eyes of the blind and ears for the deaf. Life for the dead and freedom for captives. The great Eddie Izzard once described the church as a place full of people with no muscles in their arms. Well, wake up, cause I've come to put the muscles back.'

Now that would have been fine, he read it perfectly, clear as a bell. The problem was – it wasn't the reading they'd chosen, and then he capped it by saying, 'Today, what you've just heard is starting to come true. Right in front of you.'

I swear he said that, like some weird old prophet or something. Like Biker John.

I think it went over most people's heads and the vicar's sermon after it was so muddled and full of incomprehensible phrases no one would have guessed Josh had read the wrong bit. But what was going on? What was he thinking of, stepping up to the mic like that and volunteering to read when we were supposed to be keeping our heads down? It wasn't karaoke night, for goodness' sake. What had happened in those years working away with his old man, and in that strange month when he disappeared and came back all beaten up?

After the service, there was the usual photos and handshaking and backslapping. But people kept coming up to Josh and muttering about what he'd said. Most of 'em seemed worried about him, taking him to one side and talking low in his ear, as if he needed help. Yet he looked fine. Better than ever. If anyone was nuts it was me, not him. But it scared me, I didn't like unplanned stuff like that. Next thing you knew, he'd be shoving me into the spotlight, and I wasn't having any of that.

Booze

When we got to the Granada, things settled down again. The Granada's a big old whitewashed hotel tucked away in the woods in a little place called Illogan. It's off a country lane that winds like an old snake. On a good day you can sit outside in the courtyard and sup in the sun. It was that kind of day. I sat in the shade with Si and Jimmy, none of us making small talk, while Jack and Josh muttered head-to-head in a sun-drenched corner. We'd gone ahead, leaving the key players to get in the photos. After a while, the wedding party appeared in big limos and said 'Hi' and 'Bye' and went on in for food and more backslapping. I dozed and left Jimmy and Si to stare each other out.

I must have fallen asleep because I woke up. Josh's mum had appeared and was bending his ear about the lack of alcohol. Not something I would have thought she'd have noticed, being teetotal herself, but she was pretty insistent about the problem, like it was Josh's fault.

'You can do something,' she kept saying, over and over.

I caught sight of Si and Jack and Jimmy grinning at each other. If nothing else, they were united in their enjoyment of seeing Josh squirm. Poor guy.

'Look, Mum, stop pressuring me. I can think for myself. I'm not a little boy now, you know.'

Pressuring him about what? He could hardly nip out and bring back a lorry load of booze for the bridegroom.

Josh's mum said something I didn't catch and left him. Josh looked lost for a while and buzzed around the yard in circles like a dying fly. Then he stopped, seemed to settle on something and gestured to Jack and Jimmy. They passed a hand across their mouths, literally wiping the smiles off. Si raised his eyebrows and nodded at me, meaning – I don't know what.

Jack and Jimmy slipped inside and reappeared with a couple of wine waiters. Josh chatted to them and then said something which set them all off laughing, Josh included. I remember envying Jack and Jimmy in that moment; they had something I'd lost . . .

'You're kidding, right?' I heard Jack say.

Josh shook his head. He clearly wasn't. The waiters' faces got serious then and they went inside with the twins and Josh. Everybody looked nervous. I glanced at Josh's mum. She was the only one smiling. She looked over at me.

'What's going on?' I said.

'You'll see, Thomas,' she said. 'Just wait.'

Well, we waited so long it got the better of us. Josh and the twins didn't come back so in the end Si and me got up and went in. Everything was normal. Jack was leaning on a pillar chatting to a beautiful girl.

'What was all that about?' I said.

He offered me a brimming glass of wine.

'Taste that,' he said.

I did. It was red wine.

'Is it good?'

'Good, good? It's vintage, you doghead. Oh, by the way, remember Miz?'

The girl nodded at me.

My mouth fell open. 'Oh, you mean you're the girl they chucked in the sea . . .'

She rolled her eyes. 'Thanks for reminding me,' she said.

'You've changed a bit,' I said.

'You haven't,' she replied with a forced smile.

I had to agree with that one. 'What . . . er . . . what you up to these days?' I asked.

'I'm a lap dancer. Studying politics. What about you?'

'Politics?'

'Yea. A girl can't strip forever.' She glanced at Jack and gave him a wink. They both laughed.

'Oh! Right! Yea. Me . . . I'm . . . not doing a lot. Tried a few things, you know. Didn't really work out.'

She nodded. 'So I heard. Anyway, Jack and I are . . . *trying a few things* ourselves right now, so I don't want to be rude . . . but – there are plenty of people to chat to, Tom. Try Sal over there – she's just finished training to be a therapist – she'll sort you out.'

And that summed her up really. Never afraid to hit back, never afraid to give you the truth cold on a plate without any garnish.

'I'd better be going, then,' I said, and got out of there as fast as I could.

In the courtyard I bumped into Josh's mum.

'I told you you'd see something, didn't I?' she said.

'See what? I saw nothing.'

Now she rolled her eyes. 'You will Thomas,' she said, 'you will.'

You know the phrase – you should have been there?

Well, I was, and I still didn't know what was going on.

Carnage

'Tom, d'you want to go to the city with us on Sunday?'

'Why?'

'Well, Josh's organising a day out, mate. Could be a laugh.'

We were in the clearing, Nat, Andy and me. I was operating the trap so they could shoot down the clay pigeons. It was like everything was speeding up, like the DVD was on fast play. One thing was racing after another.

'What's going on?' I said, throwing down the clay disc. It shattered on the dirt floor.

'Easy!' said Nat. 'Those things are expensive.'

'Well, stop shooting 'em to pieces, then,' I muttered.

Nat and Andy glanced at one another.

'Look,' I said, 'what's going on? How come Josh is suddenly organising trips for us?'

'D'you not wanna go, then?' said Andy.

'I don't know, what's gonna happen? Tea and buns in the park? A Happy Meal in the high street?'

Andy sighed, broke his gun and leant it against a tree.

'Tom,' he said, 'we're just a few mates doing stuff. That's all. If you wanna come, you can.'

'But you've gotta admit,' I said, 'he is different, isn't he? Josh would never have done this before.'

Nat turned away and loaded his gun. Andy looked at me for a long time and eventually gave me the slightest of nods.

I loaded the trap and Nat blew the pigeon into a hundred clay splinters.

The city turned out to be Exeter, not London as I'd first thought.

It was the May bank holiday so the streets were jammed with tourists and day trippers.

'So we're in the city,' I said, as we fought our way out of the station. 'What now?'

Si was there, and Andy of course, and the twins Jack and Jimmy; also Nat, with some guy from the Greyhound called Matt, and Miz. Apparently she and Jack had a casual thing going on.

Josh snapped his fingers.

'Let's check out the cathedral,' he said.

'Please tell me that's the name of a pub,' I muttered as we turned and walked smack into a wall of bodies coming the other way.

It wasn't a pub. It was a big grey building sitting on a large lawn. It looked dull and difficult to me, like school. Students and kids lolled about on the grass outside. Adults snapped cameras and looked stressed. I was bored already. And I couldn't understand why no one was complaining. Why were we spending a hot bank holiday hanging around an old monument?

Josh led the way in and we stood around in the spacious foyer watching people buying tickets to go inside.

'That ain't right,' said Josh.

I said nothing. We all said nothing.

'This place was built so people could get in touch with God, right?' he said.

I don't know why he looked at me; all I could think of to do was shrug and look embarrassed.

'You know, years back there was a guy who carried two bags of dirt round with him.'

'What?'

'Yea, he dug up two patches of ground and put them in his saddlebags cause he'd met God on that little bit of the planet. He figured if he could just keep that bit of earth he'd be able to carry the Maker round with him. But s'pose God's on every bit of turf? Every rubbish tip, every battlefield, every slum, every council block and every penthouse suite – even,' and he grinned now, 'in a cathedral. S'pose every bit of turf is God's turf. What do they call it? Hallowed ground?'

I shrugged again. We all shrugged. He'd really lost us now. I just wanted a drink.

'Stay here,' he said. 'I think I saw a builder's merchant over the road.' And he went back outside.

'Oh, this is perfect,' I said. 'He brings us to a big church and scarpers.'

'Tom, shut up.'

When Si told you to shut up, you shut up.

It may only have been five minutes before he came back, but it felt like five months. We were blocking the doorway and I knew that sooner or later we'd be moved on by some old geezer in a cap and a uniform.

Eventually I spotted a couple of good-looking Japanese women and I just switched my brain onto watching them to forget the torture of the moment.

It was so effective I didn't spot Josh's return. Instead I just heard the crashing sound.

'What the. . .'

There was broken glass and money everywhere . . . Bits of silver spinning across the floor, rolling under our feet, clattering down the steps and out of the building. So many coins. Josh was scooping them up in handfuls and flinging them about. There was a sledgehammer on the floor near his feet. An alarm was wailing in the background.

That was enough for me. I was out of there.

Vice-like grip

'Tom, come back!'

I'd been running for ten minutes – and that's very impressive for me.

I hadn't been fit in a good long while – sitting in a chair and consuming lots of alcohol does not make you a long-distance runner.

I'd run across the cathedral green, down the high street, and just slowed up in a backstreet when I heard his voice. I hadn't even realised I'd been followed. And I certainly never expected him.

It was Jude. The smooth guy I'd first seen with Si and Josh in the Greyhound.

'Where did you come from?' I gasped, turning and squatting down, my hands clutching onto a drainpipe.

'I followed you guys. I'm interested in what's going on.'

Now for some reason that made me laugh, as much as you can laugh when you're coughing up your guts in an alley.

'I'm interested in what's going on, too,' I said. 'I wish someone would tell me. Weird things keep happening.'

'These are dark times, Josh, dark times. And dark times need a hero.'

'A hero?'

'Sure. You watch. This is just the beginning, Josh's on the rise. He's not the kid you thought he was.'

'I know that,' I said and I coughed again and spat a mouthful of phlegm across the ground.

'It's not going to be easy for him. He needs you, Tom. You and the others. You don't have to understand him to go with him. Just keep taking a few steps at a time.'

'You make it sound like some kind of mission.'

'It is.'

He offered me his hand and helped me up. Then he wouldn't let go of me. I noticed he was wearing a Rolex watch and more gold than I'd ever seen.

'I just want a quiet life,' I muttered, 'in fact, I don't know why I'm stood here talking to you . . .'

'Because you want something more. And because he needs you. He wants you with him. If you'll stay with it you'll see plenty of action.'

'I don't wanna see plenty of action. I just wanna sit in a dark corner and hide.'

He gripped my hand tightly.

'Listen! You're not paying attention! If you want your days to count, stick with him. Why d'you think I've been watching him? I'm fed up, too. Tired of my life. Tired of the sham and the mess. We have a chance to make a difference. To change the world.' He pushed his face close to mine and hissed out his next three words. 'To make history.'

His mouth was so close a fleck of warm spit landed on my left cheek and stuck there.

People were passing by, some of them throwing us watchful glances, but he didn't care. I did, I'd have run away, but he wouldn't let go of my hand.

'Think about it, and don't let him down.'

And he finally let go, turned and walked away.

I massaged my hand and watched Jude strut away. My hand still hurt from his vice-like grip, and I could still smell his expensive aftershave and his cigarette breath.

But it was Biker John's words that hung around in my head:

'You wanna watch this guy, big things are gonna follow in his wake . . .'

Really? I still just wanted to find a quiet, oak-beamed pub and hide in the dark.

Indiana Jones

By the time I got back to the cathedral, they'd gone. Remnants of broken glass and a few stray coins were still being swept up by disgruntled staff, but order had been restored and people were paying to see God again. I sat on the steps outside and watched for a while. Rich, fat, camera-laden tourists handed over the skimmings of their income. One or two less fortunate folk dug deep and scraped enough for the entrance fee. I wondered how many of them were on speaking terms with the Almighty. And then I laughed out loud, so loud that some of the nearby kids turned and stared.

What right did I have to ask the question? What did I know about the Supreme Being? Very little, that's what. Very little. I'd been in a church choir once. Just for a short time. Absconded when my voice broke and the girl I fancied left. I'd wanted to be in God's gang, back then

. . . whatever that meant. I mean, how were you supposed to get in? And did it really mean dressing up and looking glum? And what did Josh know about all that? Nothing. That's what. He wasn't religious. Unless he'd seen the light while he'd been away slapping paint and stippling ceilings with his old man . . . And then I saw the light – of course, that was it. That's what had happened. He'd been indoctrinated that time he dropped off the map and disappeared for a while. Probably met some nut in a cult meeting and swallowed a whole load of bonkers propaganda. No wonder he looked so rough when he got back.

But that didn't make sense. Josh was too sensible for that. And anyway, if you get religion you don't normally go and smash up your nearest cathedral. And people like Jude and Biker John don't suddenly get interested in you. They run the other way. There had to be more to it than that. Question was – did I really care? I'd been glad of his friendship, and lately I'd been watching porn less and getting out more. That's all I wanted. That was enough, a little improvement. I didn't need more. I didn't need some real-life Indiana Jones trying to make my life more exciting.

I went to find that oak-beamed pub. There was bound to be one in a place with a big cathedral.

They were all sat on the high street. Hundreds of them. Sat on the pavement, sat on the road, sat on benches, sat on top of waste bins and concrete bollards. They were everywhere. Kids, adults, teenagers, yobs, yuppies, OAPs, babies. . . And they all had one thing in common. They had burgers in their hands. There must have been a hundred of them in that crowd. Two hundred, even. On the edge a couple of guys in McDonalds's uniforms were standing shaking their heads and frowning a lot.

I thought it was just some bank holiday street party, till Miz rushed over and grabbed me. She didn't even know me and she was holding me like a long-lost boyfriend.

'He did it again!' she yelled. 'He did it again!'

And she ran off. Nat and Andy sauntered up, big grins on their faces, ketchup on their hands.

'He did what again?' I asked, knowing I'd regret it.

'I think we solved the mystery about that night at the Counterfeit Clash gig.' Nat ran a hand over his head and sighed. 'Case closed, totally,' he said and he nodded at the crowd.

'What the hell are you talking about?'

Nat held up a wedge of burger bun.

'He did it again,' he said. 'The trick with the burgers from nowhere.'

'You mean . . .' I looked at the hundreds of faces, the teeth tearing at the bread and chewing on the meat.

'Veggie burgers too,' said Andy. 'Josh thought of everything.'

'Wait, wait a minute.' I held up my hand. 'You're telling me Josh has given out free burgers to this lot? Where'd he get the money?'

'No money,' said Nat. 'Who needs money!'

'No money?'

'No money. See that kid over there, the girl with the Madonna T-shirt? He borrowed her burger and snap! He made a whole lot more.'

'Snap? Snap?! Who's he think he is now? Paul Daniels? You don't just make a hundred burgers . . .'

'Two hundred.'

'Two hundred burgers – from nothing.'

'He did.'

'What's wrong with you? Think about it. This is Josh. This is the kid who grew up round the corner from you.

His dad's a decorator, watches paint dry all day. He's just Josh. Used to sing out of tune and tackle badly in football practise. Don't come it with me about magic burgers.'

Andy placed his hands on my shoulders.

'Tom – look. These people didn't pay for this and we didn't nick it. I'm telling you. He's a genius. We got free burgers forever.'

'Then maybe he'd better come up with free money too – cause he's gonna have one hell of a bill to pay after that cathedral carnage.'

Their faces froze.

'Yea,' I said. 'Think about that one.'

And I left the high street and caught the next train back.

Fourth Bit

Opting out

I didn't see any of them for a month. I kept out of their way. I stayed at home and drank a lot. I didn't go to the clearing and I kept out of the Greyhound. I missed all the good May weather, and believe me, it was a good one, but I didn't care. No one came looking for me so I figured they'd given up on me. Whatever crusade Josh was on, I wasn't part of it. Jude had been wrong. It wasn't that important. It was easy to opt out. I'd just done it.

Then I got the letter in the post. It was from Sal. Miz's mate. The *therapist*. Another girl I didn't know getting closer than I wanted. Apparently Josh had been making up stories. Yea, I know, bonkers. But he was doing it. And according to Sal these stories had hidden messages. Oh right. Covert then. Now he's not only Indiana Jones, he's James Bond. Secret codes and nudge-nudge wink-wink stories. She thought his latest one might interest me.

Two brothers: Sam and Dave. One of them, Dave, decides to leave home. He's bored. Wants to find some adventure, some danger. Something more. (Well you got that wrong Sal – it ain't me). He talks to his old man about getting away but his dad's broken-hearted. They're a close family. Their mother died two years back and his sister's emigrated with her lover. Dad's lost enough family members. But Dave's decided, so he slips into the old man's study one night, steals his pistol from a desk drawer and waits his chance. One night a few days later, when his brother's out, Dave pulls the gun on his father and makes him hand over the family jewels. The old guy keeps a stash of heirlooms in a safe in the wall. Only he knows the combination, so Dave makes him open the safe at gunpoint and hand over the stash. His mum's wedding ring, some family diamonds, spare cash kept back for a rainy day. Well – it's raining now – cats and dogs. Dave takes off with the money, and when his father chases after him and tries to stop him on the drive there's a struggle and the gun goes off. The old man isn't hurt but the boy steps back and fires a second time. The old man crumples to the ground. Dave shuts down his emotions, turns and runs. His father has to spend two months in hospital recovering but he pulls through. Sam's furious and ready to kill his younger brother.

Dave's on the road and not taken much with him. A change of clothes. His mobile phone. His GameBoy. The usual essentials.

He makes for the best bar in town. Buys a few drinks, hires a few female friends. The drinking's good, the sex is even better. He makes a few friends, goes to a few gigs. His reputation spreads. This boy's a party animal. He meets some guys who are planning a trip to Thailand. Cool, he thinks. Now, that really is escaping. So he jumps on a plane, then gets a boat, a bus and a taxi. And suddenly he's a stranger in a strange land. He moves in with a local girl, a dancer in a club. They have a good life. Then one day she leaves him – no word, she's just gone. And so's all the money he was keeping in a tin under the bed. He finds his friends have moved on long ago. So he goes back to the club where he met his girlfriend. They don't want to know. He gets into a fight with the barman over the girl and then discovers the truth – she was a prostitute all along and he never knew it. Dave gets beaten up and thrown out into a back alley. No money, no friends. Then he meets a guy who, unbeknown to him, is a pimp. He *offers help and a bed for a few nights. Before he knows it, he's drawn into a life of prostitution. To muzzle his conscience he starts taking drugs, and to fuel the habit he has to keep on with the work. It's killing him, inside and out. He was once good-looking but the abuse is robbing him of all that. As he lies under another brutal customer he starts to think of home. This life is a million miles from the happy, creative environment he once inhabited. He thinks of his dad and he wonders. Can he go home? Can he face the recrimination? Is his father still alive anyway? Or will his brother be in charge and just throw him out on the street?*

Later that night, when he's drunk and all alone he switches on his mobile. There are two hundred and fifty-seven new messages. (No mobile can store that many, can it?) Every one is from his father. He's scared to open them and read them. He knows he's in trouble. Life is unfair; there can't be any good news waiting for him. So he stays away and never opens the messages, never discovers that his father is waiting for him, running down the road every day to see if his son is limping home, covered in mud and sores. Never finds out that his dad has a party planned for him. Instead, he stays away. And eventually he dies.

The obvious thing

I stared at the letter for a long time. I felt as if Sal was invading my space, sending me something like this. Yet, it was fascinating too. A good-looking woman takes the time to scribble a note. That has to be worth something.

Then I got a phone call.

'Who's this?'

'Josh. Who's that?'

'You know who it is, you called me.'

'Tom, I'm worried about you. How you doing?'

'I've been better.'

'Haven't seen you for a while. You haven't been in the Greyhound.'

'I didn't want to go.'

'What? A place brimming with booze . . .'

'Josh, what do you want? I'm busy . . .'

'Busy? Doing what? Watching porn?'

'Josh, I don't know what to say to you. You're different, you've changed.'

'I haven't.'

'Oh come on . . . I don't think I ever saw you magic up two hundred burgers before.'

Sigh.

'You haven't known me that long, Tom.'

'Josh – I don't know what to make of it. You smashed up a cathedral. You're weird.'

'And you're not?'

'Yea, OK, I'm weird. But I'm as strange as I always was – I've always been a loser. You've turned into Superman overnight. And what's with all the God stuff? Where d'you get religion?'

Pause.

'Look, Tom, this isn't easy for me either.'

'Really? I thought it was. I thought you could just magic up free money out of nothing. You can do anything now.'

'It's not magic, Tom. Look, I wanna talk to you about it properly. One to one . . . Meet me the day after tomorrow in the clearing. Five o'clock. OK?'

'Maybe.'

'Good.'

Click. The phone went dead.

So I did the obvious thing. I went to see my old mum and dad.

Mum had spent all her life on the go. She never sat still. If she did, she fell asleep. My old man, on the other hand, was happy to spend a lot of his life asleep – asleep or working. They were still in the same old farmhouse they'd lived in all my life, out in the sticks, half an hour from me. My dad was still doing what he'd always done, working with wood and turning it into stuff he could sell on through my uncle's shop. He built stuff, he carved stuff, and mostly these days he imported stuff. Mainly from Thailand and Laos.

As soon as I walked in the door, Mum was at me with a hug. I'd moved away to my own pad not long after escaping uni so she loved it whenever I returned with my tail between my legs. My mum is the sweetest lady in the world, and she always has fresh cakes on the go. These days it's usually muffins.

'Tom!'

She clutched me tightly and, while she was still embedded in my body, she called out, 'Shaun, your boy's back!'

She turned and waved at the hob.

'I just this minute took them out. Careful, they're hot! Where've you been? We've heard nothing.'

'Oh, still in the flat.'

'Working?'

'Sort of.'

There was a footfall behind and my dad appeared, still rubbing sleep from his eyes. It was Sunday morning so I guess he'd been dozing in front of the telly. My dad was as thin as a bootlace and a little taller than me; he had wise grey eyes and didn't waste an awful lot of energy on smiling too much.

'Tom,' he said with a cautious nod, and he walked over and shook my hand.

We had this hugely tactile kind of relationship, him and me.

'Not heard much,' he said, helping himself to a muffin.

'Careful! They're hot!' said my mum.

We both scooped up cakes and flopped opposite each other across the large kitchen table. I'd done my growing

up round that table. Games, food, friends, homework, sex
education, arm-wrestling. All the important things in life.

We battled through the heat of the muffins and
chewed on them.

'Sorted things out, then?' my dad asked.

I looked at him, chewed and wondered for a moment.

I wanted to talk to him, I wanted to talk to them both.
Obviously I couldn't tell them about the booze and the
porn, but I wanted to sound them out about Josh. They'd
remember him. They'd tell me what to do. At least I told
myself they would.

'Dad,' I said, avoiding the incendiary question about
work, and my lack of it, 'I . . . er . . . I wanted to tell you
something. I've got to know this guy a bit . . .'

He raised a single eyebrow and sat back in his seat,
and every single bit of the movement megaphoned one
question: 'You're not gay, are you?'

I laughed but he scowled.

'No, Dad, anything but.'

'Remember Julie from the next farm? She's moved in
with another woman,' my mother added helpfully.
'They're always together.'

'Yea, Mum, it's not that.' I thought for a moment. 'It's
Josh, remember him?'

My dad brightened. 'Joe's lad? Yea! Joe's still doing
well. Business on the up . . . that's something you could
get into. Ask him. Ask Josh if you can apprentice with
his dad.'

'Well, he did give me some help a few years back,
when I was thinking about trying to start a business.'

'I remember. What happened to that idea?'

I shrugged. 'Oh . . . something else came along.'

'And what happened to that?'

This was not going well.

'Dad, I just want some advice.'

'That's all you ever want, isn't it? Don't want to work, just want to consider the options. It's a real world out there. You can't sponge forever, Tom.'

'I'm not sponging.' Which, of course, was a blatant lie.

'I never understood why you gave up university,' my mum said, and suddenly we were back in the land of *I've heard this one a thousand times before.*

'Mum, you know why, it wasn't me.'

'It wasn't easy,' said Dad. 'You had a rough time, we understand that. But you've got to apply yourself. Mike applied himself. I often wonder what he'd be doing.'

'I know, Dad, you told me. Many times.'

'It's not too late to make a go of it.'

No, but it was too late to try and sort anything out now. We were back on old ground, ground littered with barbed memories and hidden bits of emotional broken glass.

'I don't know why we can't get past this,' I sighed.

'Tell us about Josh,' said Mum.

'Really? Oh, OK. Well, I've fallen in with him and a few of his mates. We just hang around together and . . .'

And I couldn't put the rest into words. There was a world of chaos raging in my head, but on paper it just looked like a few mates hanging together.

I stood up. 'I fancy a stroll,' I said. 'Need to just get my head clear a bit. Want to come?'

'I'll get some lunch going.'

'Dad?'

He shook his head. 'Got some things to do.'

So that was that. I strolled down to the mill by the river and did what I've often done when my head's full of frustration. I lobbed stones for half an hour. When you've lived with people all your life, why's it so difficult to communicate with them? And why did it always come back to Mike?

The red chameleon

'Why d'you smash up a big church for no reason?'

'It wasn't for no reason.' Pause. 'Churches like that keep people away.'

'Away from what?'

'Away from life.'

'What?'

Josh threw a can in the air and lobbed a stone at it. He missed. So he tried again and hit it this time. We were in the clearing behind the Old Mariner, just the two of us.

'Those places are supposed to be a gateway for the world,' he said, 'not some exclusive members-only club.'

'Where d'you get this stuff from?'

He frowned.

'What stuff?' he asked.

'This . . . I dunno . . . all-seeing wisdom you've suddenly got. This . . . changing the planet stuff.'

A grin snaked across his lips like a thin red chameleon.

'From . . . it sort of began with my cousin.'

'Biker John?'

He nodded.

'We sat on a kerb one day when we were twelve and made a pact.'

'And now he's in prison.'

The chameleon slipped away from his face.

'Yep.' He scooped a handful of sandy earth and weighed it in his fist.

'But I don't get it – it's like one minute you're just one of the lads, all matey, helping me fill out forms. The next you're Gandhi, or Superman, or Al Gore. Wanting to save the world. You're nuts.'

He pursed his lips. 'You haven't known me that long, Tom. You have to cut me some slack.'

'What, and not think you've got some obsessive, Michael Jackson Messiah-fixation going on?'

He sighed. 'Something like that, yea. Tom, you're not gonna like this, and you'll wonder who I am to say it but . . . you gotta change the CD, mate.'

'What?'

'While you got the old CD still playing in that head of yours you'll never get what's going on. You gotta change track. More than that – you gotta begin again. Get a fresh pint. The old one's flat and stale.'

CDs? Pints?

'What the hell are you talking about?'

'When you video one of your late night porn channels, you just tape over the old programmes, right?'

'Yea.'

'Get a new tape, Tom. Brand new, clean start. Don't keep re-using the old tapes, cause you got all that history still playing in the background. Don't get me wrong – the old stuff is useful. It's life. But sometimes you need a clean break. A fresh start.'

If I'm honest he spooked me then, something inside got really scared, yet I didn't know why cause I wasn't really sure what he was on about. I guess I projected onto his words all that I didn't wanna hear right there and then. And suddenly it was just like school again. Do this, don't do that. All that I hated about teachers and parents and the pressure to succeed. I thought he was my friend, but it was like he was the Bill, leaning on me. Making me conform. I didn't want that. I didn't tell him though. I just got up and left him with his fist-ful of sand.

I drank a lot in the next weeks and, in spite of his advice, I kept re-using the old tapes. I ate a lot of Marmite as well. Always loved Marmite as a kid and it felt safe, felt like something that was reassuring. And I dug out my old vinyl, too. Records we'd had kicking around since I was a kid. Seventies pop, mostly, songs that reminded me of a time when life was OK, when I hadn't failed too many exams and too many people. Days of riding round on bikes with your coat hooked on your head, flying behind you like Superman's cape. When our family was four and not three. And my dad smiled a lot. When the future was something to look forward to, something to relish. Just listening to those old songs crackle and hiss under the needle made me feel better. Like everything was normal again. Like the ground wasn't constantly shifting under my feet. As I said, reassuring. Just as well, because Josh was about to drag me right off to some-place very shaky indeed.

The biggest minefield in the world

'I got tickets for south-east Asia.'

Josh eyed the lot of us and grinned as he dropped his bombshell.

I hadn't seen the lot of them in weeks. In the end, Andy came looking for me and dragged me off to the clearing where there was a dozen of 'em hanging around. I'd heard that Jack and Jimmy had jacked in their business – Mama Kray had hired a couple of skater punks to take over and mind the shop while her pre-cious boys went AWOL. Must have cost her an arm and a leg and a couple of ribs. It was all getting out of hand. Si was there, pacing and frothing at the mouth.

'You're kidding, right?'

Si was having none of it. He'd never been out of Cornwall.

'I want you to see some life,' Josh insisted. 'More than this, I mean.'

'Where in south-east Asia?'

Josh pondered for a minute, then crouched in the clearing and slashed a few curves in the sand, like he was drawing a map. He jabbed a stick in one corner.

'Cambodia,' he said. 'Land of the old Khmer Empire.'

'Yea, and a million landmines.'

'Better watch where you step, then.'

As I slipped through the fence and out of the clearing, a hand gripped my shoulder. I started and glanced round. It was Jude. Where the hell had he come from? I hadn't seen him in the clearing. Had he been lurking between the trees somewhere?

'You should go,' he said. 'You should really go. Stuff'll happen out there and no one'll be the same. He'll prove himself, and when he does, people'll take notice. Big people, important people. People who really can help save the planet. You'd be a loser to stay home.'

'I'll be a loser wherever I go,' I said. 'Besides, I don't have money for the jabs and all the extra stuff.'

'You do now,' he said, shoving his face close to mine.

As he walked away I could still smell the aftershave and cigarettes lingering in the air and, when I pushed my hand in my jacket pocket, my fingers jabbed into a wad of notes. Now I had no excuse.

Like a dead leaf

'Cambodia. Land of Death and Glory. Angkor Wat. Pol
Pot. Killing Fields and Khmer temples. Mystical, forgotten jewel, a damaged precious stone, once the pearl of
south-east Asia, now the home of two million dead in a
thousand mass graves.'

'Shut up, Matt.'

'Just reading what it says here.'

'Well, don't.'

Matt shrugged, pulled out his iPod and started groaning along to the Scissor sisters.

Jack pressed his nose against the glass of the plane
window and studied the ground below. Water buffalo
and rice paddies cross-faded into half-finished buildings
and streets of cyclo-taxis and minibuses. Tiny people sat
in crowds on mopeds, bicycles and trucks.

Stepping off that plane was like walking into a burning building. The heat tore into you like a bad case of flu.
It assaulted your body and left you doused in sweat in a
matter of seconds. We escaped from jumpers and jackets
and hid behind sharp designer shades. Actually, I got
mine in a little village garage somewhere but the paper
ticket on the arm claimed that Steve McQueen once
wore a pair like this. Yea, right. We stood there blinded
by the light, a straggle of guys, Sal, Miz and a few of
their mates. And, of course, Josh. He pointed towards
the air terminal and we limped across the tarmac (where
were the gleaming steel escalators and carpeted arrivals
lounge?) to a building which bore the sign Pochentong
Airport. It was about the size of a bus station and had all
the charm of a church hall. Soldiers hung around not
smiling. Officials took our passports and said a lot of
things to each other about us. Didn't understand a single word. Eventually, Josh handed over some money, we

got our passports back and we went looking for our luggage. I felt sick and confused. Sitting in a plane for fifteen hours had left me feeling like I'd just spent the night in a tumble dryer. I trailed behind the others like a dead leaf stuck to the bottom of Josh's shoe. I'd no choice now. If I didn't stick with these guys I really would be lost.

Fifth Bit

Rotting corpses

From that day on, it was like we moved into top gear. Things were never the same again after we arrived in Phnom Penh. Josh knew what he was doing and the rest of us did not have a clue. He was like Holmes and we were a dozen Dr Watsons. He was Eric Morecambe, we were Ernie Wise. How long he'd been planning this was anybody's guess, but he looked like he was born for this place.

Outside the airport, a hundred taxi drivers showered us with a hail of Khmer. Jack and Jimmy tried communicating with them using all the swear words in the English language and a few new ones they made up, but that was about as useful as putting George Bush in the White House. Si waded in and threatened to chin a few of them, and the size of him did shut a few of them up. But it was Josh who seemed to find a third language that worked. Some pidgin dialect that made sense to him, them, and not us. He struck a deal with two drivers, handed over the cash and before you could say Mekong Delta we were bundled in two buses and headed for a hotel. As we wound through the city I stared into the great river running beside the road and imagined gunboats patrolling

it, picking off dissenters and anyone who was 'educated'
– anyone who owned a pen or wore glasses.

Apparently the Mekong had once been flush with rotting corpses and bloated bodies, in the days when Pol
Pot had turned the entire country into his own concentration camp.

The buses pulled up and Josh leapt out and
announced that we were at the Foreign Correspondents
Club of Cambodia. He led the way up some stairs and
we ended up huddled round a table for twenty, supping
a beer that went by the name of Tiger; big strong guys
cowering under huge wooden fans from the fifties, and
tiny, flitting geckos with detachable tails. After the
clammy heat outside it was relatively cool and there
was a buzz of European chatter that made it all seem a
little more like home. We ate western food and made
eyes at Miz and Sal and their mates. It was all beginning
to feel OK again. Then Josh sparked up and spoilt
everything.

Putting on the vinyl

'Guys, you gotta change the record.'

I threw Josh a quick wounded glance but he wasn't
staring directly at me.

'It's like the way music's gone – you can't play vinyl
on a CD player and you can't jam a CD into an iPod. It
just doesn't work. The technology's moved on. But the
music's all good. Old and new. You just need to adapt
and change the way you play it as the world moves on.
It's easy to get stuck on the old. A lot of people love the
old, they know what's safe and they wanna still play
their old records. But things change. Life changes.
People change. And as for God – '

'God?' Jimmy recoiled as he said it. 'Why you talking about God?'

'What did you think this was all about?'

'I dunno. You just seem a cool guy. You never said this was about religion. If it is, I'm going home.'

'You see, you're doing it again.'

'Doing what?' snapped Jack.

'Thinking in the old ways – putting on the vinyl records.'

This time he did throw me a glance.

'Just because a bunch of people claim to have the corner on faith and turn it into something old and dull and ridiculous – d'you think that matters?'

'I thought you wanted to save the planet,' said Andy, 'you know – fix the environment.'

'I wanna fix your environment. Or rather I want you to do it. You can all do it.'

'Now you sound like Oprah Winfrey,' said Jimmy.

'Listen!' He stood up and slapped a hand on the table; a dozen beers slopped across the surface, a couple of geckos ran for their lives overhead and a handful of other European customers sat back in their seats and started to enjoy the show.

'God is like the internet. Where is it? You can't see it, you can't touch it – yet you get the benefits. Does it exist? Yes. Where is it? Somewhere. Everywhere. Can you hold it in your hand? No. It's beyond you. You know it's there because of what it gives you. You could argue there is no internet – but you still go on benefiting from it. Well, wake up – cause God's like that. He's everywhere, he's huge and he ain't going away. And you're part of him, in the same way that the internet is full of pages. It's as if you're all web pages. The Creator's web pages.' He pressed a clammy fist to his forehead and scowled. We just stared. Blankly.

Nat raised a finger. 'Are you making this up or did you read it in a book?' he asked. Josh ignored the question.

'OK, think of this – the internet is massive, right? Like . . . like the temples we're gonna see. They stretch forever – but they're all made of little bricks. Or . . . or think of the paddy fields we saw from the plane. Acres of 'em. Too big to get your head round. But each one is made up of little tiny rice plants that you can sit in the palm of your hand. Each brick is a vital part of the temple, each rice plant makes up the field. All unique, all different. So although the internet is colossal, it's small too – because it's just made up of single pages. Each one unique and different. And each of you is like one of God's pages – whether you like it or not, you say something to the world. About humanity, about life and yes – about the Creator. So what are you gonna say? What will be on your website? And where you gonna find the inspiration?'

He sat down again and we didn't know what to say. I thought I'd understood about every third word so I ordered some more beers and we broke up into little groups and drank some more. I wandered over to the huge glassless window and leant on the concrete, gazing into the Mekong River for a while. Something about it calmed me. This little bit of water that was part of the massive delta. I felt a hand on my shoulder and turned. It was him again – Jude. He always seemed to be on my shoulder when I felt like running.

'What d'you want? And don't grip my shoulder like that . . . please.'

Jude smiled and let go.

'Most people pass through history,' he said. 'This is history.'

'What?'

'Don't give up on this, Tom. I got a hunch the next few days will change us all. Hang on a bit longer and the pieces will fall into place.'

'I don't know what I'm doing here.'

'You're doing what we're all doing here. Trotting along like a bunch of strays hoping for a bone.'

'What?'

'Beggars looking for food.'

And it was odd he said that, cause we were about to encounter an awful lot of beggars in the next week.

A bunch of Homers

'You brought a gun to Cambodia?' Andy stared at Nat in total disbelief. 'There are creatures in the toilet here higher up in the gene pool than you.'

We were in our hotel room in the Goldiana – a five-star palace with a gym, a swimming pool and the tariff of a youth hostel. And rooms with three beds and a minibar so guys like me, Nat and Andy could kip down together. Nat was walking about the place in his boxers, brandishing an old .22 Webley service revolver and looking for all the world like Dirty Harry.

'You know there are still guys round here who blow people's heads off for a living,' Andy went on, 'and with guns ten times that size.'

'So?'

'So how did you get it through customs?' Andy demanded.

'Luck, dude, luck,' he said.

'You realise if there had been another bomb scare we'd all still be in Heathrow with Her Majesty's finest shining torches up our backsides. You could have blown the whole trip. What you gonna do with it anyway? Shoot clay at Angkor Wat?'

'Maybe. Never know when you might need one. Place like this, man – you could be facing worst case scenario times a thousand. Straight up, dude, straight up. Total carnage.'

'Nat – you don't know what you're talking about,' said Andy. 'You meet any bad guys out here – you're dead. Dead! They orchestrated genocide. One little pop-gun ain't gonna bother them.'

'Whatever, dude,' he said. 'Whatever.'

'Nat,' I said, 'please don't do anything stupid.'

He shrugged. 'If I do,' he replied, 'you'll be the first to know.'

Andy stuck his head out of the window and stared at the bustle below. The smell of jack fruit and root ginger wafted in from outside amidst the jangle of funeral chimes and chattering children.

'Who is he?' he muttered.

'Who d'you mean?' I said.

'Josh. I thought I knew him – but he's changed. And why's he dragged us all this way out here?'

Nat grinned and aimed his revolver at the back of the door.

'I like it. It's an adventure. I never been travelling before. Soak it up, man, it'll be over too soon.'

Jude stepped out of the bathroom. I'd not even seen him come in.

'How long you been in there?' I snapped.

He ignored the question. He was still dressed in too much black gear, in spite of the heat.

'What bothers me,' he said, lowering himself precisely onto my bed (he did everything with precision), 'what bothers me is it seems like something significant is going down here – but where are the cameras? Who's going to tell the rest of the world?

'What d'you mean, significant?'

Jude pulled a bush knife from inside his ankle boot and carefully picked at his nails with it.

'Where d'you get that?' asked Andy. 'Grief, why's everyone feel the need to be armed out here? It's like going on holiday with the X-men!'

'Well, we're certainly a bunch of freaks,' Jude said. 'But to backtrack to your question – can't you guys see it? Grief, you all seem so blind. You bumble along like a posse of Homer Simpson clones, while all around bushes are burning and voices are booming and you don't see it and you can't hear it. This is the time of your life, dudes, open your eyes. Josh is going to change the world. And I mean the world. It'll never be the same again.' He paused and studied our blank faces. 'I wonder what the collective noun is for a bunch of Homers – a vacuum probably. Why the hell did he sidle up to you lot?'

Andy was the one doing the sidling right then.

'Jude, I don't know what sewer he'd fallen in when he tripped over you – but you'd better watch that mouth of yours, or it'll be on the wrong end of a baseball bat. I hate you, mate – I don't even know you and I can't stand you.'

'Andy, back off,' Nat said.

But Jude raised a calm hand.

'It's OK. You'll thank me one day, Andy, when we're no longer subject to short-sighted governments who suck up to corrupt European powerbrokers. But don't worry – I won't even say "I told you so"; in fact, from now on, I won't offend you with my thoughts. Just watch and learn boys, watch and learn.'

Jude stood up slowly, threw me a genuine smile and was gone in three steps. He didn't even slam the door, it just closed with the gentlest click in the world.

A lifetime of free booze

Jack and Jimmy appeared a moment later. No knock at the door or inquisitive peep round the wood – they just came straight on in, faces as dark as a bad bruise, expressions as raw as an open wound. They weren't happy.

'Oh, he's smart, isn't he?' said Jimmy, tearing open the fridge and ripping out two little bottles of whisky.

'What d'you mean?' Andy snapped. 'And that's our drink.'

'What do I mean? What do I mean! He lulls us into some false reality about being a cool dude and a good mate and it's all "How's the poker and how's the surfin'?" Then as soon as he's got us out here and we can't get away he tells us he's starting some new cult and we're the congregation. Well, no thanks very much, mate. I'm outta here. As soon as we get back home, I'm gone. You won't see me for surf.'

'You knew he was weird, though,' said Andy.

'When?' Jack eyed Andy and their eyes locked, both of them refusing to blink.

'When he came looking for you in the first place. I mean, who does that? Who comes knockin' on your door saying, "Hey, I got a better deal for you – wanna come try it?" You must have been bigger suckers than you look if you thought this was about selling Amway.'

'Andy – you should be careful,' said Jack, 'big brother ain't around right now.'

Jack took a step towards Andy. They were of equal height, and neither of them as muscled as their brothers, but Jack had a hint of violence in his stance, and Andy couldn't square up to that.

'Easy ladies,' Nat said. 'Chill dudes, chill.'

For a moment no one moved. Then Jimmy cracked a knuckle and Nat cleared his throat.

'Hey, I got a question – is it right that you dudes gave up working?' Nat asked. 'I mean, that's like totally not normal.'

Jimmy jabbed a threatening finger at Nat and said, 'What would you know about normal?' and he followed it with enough swearing to make the Sex Pistols raise a collective pin-pierced eyebrow.

Andy grinned suddenly, a mile-wide smile tinged with put-down. 'I bet it's costing your old dear a packet to finance this little dump in the woods. She's had to hire replacements for you two, hasn't she?'

Jack shook his head very slowly. He wasn't smiling.

'You leave her out of this.'

He cussed and placed his leather boot on Andy's left trainer. His face hardened as he ground the other guy's foot beneath his own. Andy said nothing but his face showed the pain. Jimmy meanwhile had grabbed Nat by the collar of his T-shirt.

'Jack,' I said, in an effort to break the tension, 'why did she let you go in the first place? I mean, it's the family business an' all.'

'Cause we told her to – and you're playing with the big boys now,' Jimmy said to me, 'so speak when you're spoken to.'

'You wouldn't say that if Si was here,' Nat said.

'Shut up!' Jimmy said and he clutched Nat's cheek in his fist and twisted the skin in his hands. Nat pulled away and let out a yelp.

Jimmy snorted, picked up his whisky and knocked it back.

'I'm gonna have words with her when we get home,' he said.

Jack snapped his head round to look at his brother and, in the same moment, Andy tore his foot free and stepped back.

'What d'you mean?' Jack said.

'Well, she could have stopped us, she's been round the block a few times. She must see through Josh.'

'Maybe she heard about the wedding,' said Nat, 'and wants a lifetime of free booze.'

'Free booze?' I said.

Andy nursed his foot and smiled. 'Ask Josh,' he said.

Suddenly Jack let out a guttural yell. I thought he was about to attack one of us but instead he slumped on Andy's bed.

'Agh!' He grabbed his head with his hands and wrestled with his scalp. 'Why's he talking like this? Why's he doing this to us?'

'Who?'

'Josh! Why's he messing with our heads, talking like he owns the planet or something? I don't get it, he was just one of us. What's he up to? Where did all this street preachin' psychobabble come from? It's like we've been set up. This wasn't supposed to happen, I thought this was about something else.'

Jimmy groaned and shook his head vehemently but he didn't offer a reply. For a moment the twins seemed completely out of their depth.

'What d'you mean?' I said.

Jack looked at me and his face softened for a moment.

'I thought we were going somewhere. Not . . . down the toilet . . .'

Jack turned away and spotted the gun.

'What the frig's that?'

Nat beamed. 'I brought my gun.'

Jack scooped it up. 'I'll have that, then.'

'What?'

'Cambodia's a dangerous place, mate. Haven't you heard? There's still guerrilla action up north. And where are we going in two days? Up north. Any old Khmer

Rouge operative takes a pop at me, I'll have him. It's just what I need to burn up some aggression right now.'

Nat looked like Jack had just eaten his winning lottery ticket. But he didn't argue; Jack and Jimmy wouldn't have had that. Jimmy helped himself to a couple more bottles from the fridge and they swaggered out.

Nat swore and threw himself across his bed. He shouldn't have done it, the bed wasn't up to the strain and two of the legs splintered and gave out. Nat's body lurched off the side and his chin connected with the floor.

'Not your day, Nat,' said Andy, as the other guy mopped blood from his swollen lips.

Anything but sleep

We did anything but sleep that night. Nat chain-smoked. Andy read cheap books he'd picked up at the airport. I opted for turning over and over in bed and sighing a lot. The place was like an oven, but when we put on the air conditioning it roared like a wounded animal. In the wee small hours we gave up and started supping beer and every other drink in our fridge. We swapped bad jokes and tried to outdo each other with stories of life's bad experiences. I ended up nicking a soul-searing read from Andy entitled *Voices from S-21: Terror and History in Pol Pot's Secret Prison* – it documented the horrors of life in a Cambodian jail. I decided I was never gonna visit that place – ever.

Sleepless and with eyes like cardboard we wandered down to breakfast, the air thick with the smell of fried eggs, fresh fruit, root ginger and street garbage. As we moved bits of food around our plates twenty small faces pressed against the window, kids selling newspapers and offering taxi rides. Every one of them had eyes that would melt granite. Hun, one of the bus drivers, appeared, and shooed the kids away. Josh appeared by the window next to Hun – he'd been out somewhere on his own already.

'Come on, I wanna take you somewhere,' he mouthed at us through the glass.

Everyone looked tired and no one was over-keen to set off on some magical mystery tour – but the girls were going so that was some consolation. I still harboured hopes of chatting up Sal; if nothing else, she had at least shown some interest in me. And any guy's allowed to misinterpret that as a sign of true love.

We boarded the buses, Jimmy and Jack sullen and simmering, Si and Andy bragging about things they'd never done. The next minutes passed in a palm-treed blur as we took the road into Phnom Penh. As we neared the heart of the city, a steady stream of mopeds poured past us like a cloud of metallic mosquitoes, weaving either side of the buses. Entire families sat aboard the bikes, tiny children standing in foot-wells clutching at the steering column and the legs of the adults for dear life. Most of the women sat side-saddle and, though the bikes veered and swerved at all imaginable angles through the onslaught of traffic, none of the passengers batted an eyelid.

Oxygen

We drew up outside a white-walled set of buildings. Barbed wire still sat around the top of a high perimeter wall. My heart picked up speed. Something wasn't right.

'What is this?' I asked as we disembarked.

A lone beggar sat in front of the gate and a couple of soldiers stood smoking nearby. Josh paid the woman on the gate. She offered to be our guide but he declined.

'What is this?' I asked again.

'Steel yourself, Tom,' Josh said. 'This won't be the eas-iest of days.'

I wanted to grab him and pull him back, stop him from leading us inside the compound. A flash of black and white raced into my head; I'd just seen a photo of this, only hours before. This was that prison, that place I vowed I'd never visit.

'Welcome to Tuol Sleng, guys,' Josh said, and he was in before I could stop him.

He clearly had no idea what he was getting us into. He'd clearly not read *Voices from S-21*.

My stomach felt like it had a loose propeller in it, I wasn't even over the trauma of a fifteen-hour flight and a night with no sleep. Now here we were plunging into the lowest level of hell itself.

Inside the outer wall a quadrant of buildings bor-dered a grassy square. Josh read the preamble in English, it was printed on a board by the entrance and introduced us to S-21: The Museum of Crime.

'During the reign of the Khmer Rouge Phnom Penh was empty, all the cities were. The place was a ghost town peopled only by those in power who were privi-leged enough to walk the streets here. The only other visitors to the capital were reluctant ones, prisoners brought to Tuol Sleng, codenamed S-21, one of a multi-tude of prisons and execution grounds in operation at that time. This place was the hub, the heart of the slaughtering machine. Anyone brought here did not survive. And,' Josh added, 'that included one Englishman.'

We walked on in odd silence, the guys frowning, the girls hanging on to each other; I couldn't work out what the hell he was playing at, bringing us here. If he wanted to wallow in this mire that was his lookout. Why take us with him? Halfway round the quad we came to a sign listing the chilling rules of confinement, The Security Regulations. They had been translated into broken English for the western tourists. We read in silence.

The Security Regulations

1. *You must answer accordingly to my questions. Don't turn them away.*
2. *Don't try to hide the facts by making pretexts this and that. You are strictly prohibited to contest me.*
3. *Don't be a fool for you are a chap who dare to thwart the revolution.*
4. *You must immediately answer my questions without wasting time to reflect.*
5. *Don't tell me either about your immoralities or the essence of the revolution.*
6. *While getting lashes or electrification you must not cry at all.*
7. *Do nothing, sit still and wait for my orders. If there is no order, keep quiet. When I ask you to do something, you must do it right away without protesting.*
8. *Don't make pretexts about Kampuchea Krom in order to hide your jaw of traitor.*
9. *If you don't follow all the above rules, you shall get many many lashes of electric wire.*
10. *If you disobey any point of my regulations you must get either ten lashes or five shocks of electric charge.*

Josh and the others passed the sign and went on into the former single cells where metal beds and rusting irons sat on display, but I kept away from the shadowed enclosures and stayed outside in the morning sun. After a while Andy and Sal re-emerged, sober-faced, and we moved on to the third side of the square, where detainees had been held in communal cells. Here wire mesh had been fitted at first floor level to prevent attempted suicides. I stood in the doorway to the first hall on the ground floor and stared at the tiny, badly constructed brick cubicles, barely large enough to turn around in, each one a former isolation cell. In the fourth block of buildings a huge chessboard of photographs displayed the faces of the dead and the missing while graphic paintings depicted the horrific sufferings that once constituted a part of daily life here. My eyes fell on a painting of two guards carrying a prisoner between them, stripped and suspended upside-down on a bamboo pole, nothing more than a bloody carcass. I think the tethered figure was a man, but for all the world it could have been a woman; male or female, they might well have been an animal as far as the captors were concerned. Enough.

I went back outside and thought about anything but this place. Nat was out there smoking, Miz and Sal were whispering to each other, their eyes wet and red. We stood in silence and listened to the sound of nearby birds, grateful that they still sang when there was so little to sing about. I hated crying. I wasn't one for sobbing and wailing. Not me. But something was welling up inside, some spectre of grief was stirring and raising its ugly head. Keep thinking of something else, Tom, keep the beast at bay. That's what I told myself. And that's what I did. I was in real danger here, teetering on the verge of breaking down in public in this dreadful, wounded place.

Josh and the others emerged into the sunlight, their faces grim. Josh started to tell Nat something he'd overheard one of the guides say, but his voice broke before he could finish the account and we all just bit our lips and left that place in silence. Even Andy and Si. Hun didn't ask any questions as we bundled clumsily aboard the buses. And, as we pulled away, and I looked back at the bleak white buildings, the single beggar by the gate raised his arm and gave me a soft, departing wave, as if to say, 'Did you see . . . Did you see . . .'

As we drove past the myriads of living, breathing Cambodians I had to remind myself that life here still went on, that people were alive. They'd survived and gone on to have children and lives and work and some kind of future. Incredibly, in spite of the darkness wrought by a million deaths, the light still burned brightly in the streets of Phnom Penh.

'This life is full of problems. Trouble's like oxygen – it's everywhere.'

Josh spoke cautiously.

We were now standing in the Killing Fields, in a place called Choeung Ek – one of a hundred burial grounds outside the city where victims had been bludgeoned to death and buried in mass graves. The place was a mottled mass of pits with little signs protruding. '*100 bodies found here*' . . . '*50 headless corpses here*'.

'You know, God is in all of life – especially the troubled places. People want him to make it all right but it doesn't work like that. Choice has complicated the world. Freedom has muddied the waters. But just because evil reigns sometimes – it doesn't signify the absence of God. If there's no light at the end of the tunnel it's not because there is no light – it's because the tunnel is buckled and twisted.'

And then Josh cried.

I couldn't believe it. He fell on his knees and sobbed in front of us. I mean, what the hell was he thinking of? We were just tourists, just a bunch of rookies hanging around in a field of holes. It wasn't our war that had murdered these people, they weren't our blunt instruments and we had no relatives here. But he sobbed and sobbed, and then, oh great, the girls joined in and, to crown it all, one or two of the other guys. Andy, even Nat. Thankfully, Jimmy looked as cool as ever but Jack looked strained, like he was training to hold back a crumbling dam. I'd never seen him like that. Si stared at the ground and eventually went off for a walk. I turned away and studied the scenery.

Part of the shocking, gut-churning truth about S-21, the detention centre, was that it had been right in the heart of the city, just another school in another street beside houses and traffic and normal day-to-day living. It had neighbours and passers-by. Out here, things were different. The Killing Fields were tranquil, pastoral even, and set out in the lonely beauty of the Khmer country-side. You could stage a picnic here.

Eventually Josh looked up, snot smeared across his face.

'I wish people could find the way of peace. But it'll go on and on. Killing, torture, rape, abuse. City after city will be attacked and traumatised. Village after village will be plundered and the children stolen and sold. It was never meant to be like this. People blame God and forget the pain that wracks his heart and head. When he planted a garden in Eden, there was no agenda for this. People weren't designed to withstand this.'

He wiped his face on his shirt and stumbled away between the empty craters. We stood around looking for some words to fill the silence. But there weren't any.

Eventually we all dispersed and I found a bit of ground and lay down in the sun.

When I stood up half an hour later I discovered I'd been lying in another mass grave.

Never gonna be good

Back in the hotel, I stood under the shower for a long time. I mean a long time. It seemed as if the stench of death would last for decades. In the end I had to come out cause Andy and Nat were stinking and needing showers too. I changed and wandered around the hotel corridors. But then I got spooked. Everywhere I went I started to see soldiers in black outfits with red checked scarves and guns. I eventually found my way to a balcony where I sat astride an oddly placed exercise bike and stared at a group of smartly dressed girls doing school on the pavement below. I started when I heard a footfall behind me – but it wasn't a black-suited killer. It was Sal; goodness' knows how she found me, but I was glad she had.

'Why d'you send me that letter?' I blurted out.

She backed up a step.

'Hey,' she said, 'what's up with you?'

I lied. I told her I was tired. I noticed she had a book in her hand.

'What you reading – *Pride and Prejudice*?'

She laughed. 'Hardly.' She held it up and read the title: *First They Killed My Father*.

'Sounds a right laugh,' I said.

'It's about Loung Ung, a five-year-old Cambodian girl who lived through the Khmer Rouge.'

I scowled. 'Think I'd rather read Jane Austen,' I said.

'So would I, or Nick Hornby maybe – but you can't hide from what happened. If today meant anything . . .'

'Today was a nightmare,' I snapped. 'I don't know what the hell I'm doing here. Do you?'

'Know what I'm doing here, or what you're doing here?'

'Both, either.'

'Well, maybe it's easier for me.' She smiled shyly. 'You see, I believe in all this anyway.'

'Believe in all what? Torture and death?'

'I meant – his stuff. What Josh has been saying. I think it makes a lot of sense. I've been waiting for someone like him. I think a lot of people have. That's why I want to be a therapist. I want to help people . . .'

'Religion's a crutch.'

'Maybe. Everyone uses crutches. Beauty, wealth, football. We all need something.'

'Stop trying to convert me.'

'You're angry, aren't you? Is it me? Or him? You see, for me this is nothing new. Well, it is in some ways, I suppose. I've never met anyone like him before. But it's not frightening.'

'Who said it's frightening? I'm not frightened.'

She flashed a bigger, wider smile.

'Course you're not, big boy,' she said and she squeezed my arm.

It's those moments when you wish you'd spent the last three years working out instead of watching porn. And the thought of that made me wince.

'What?'

'I'm not a good person, Sal.'

'Who is?'

You are, I wanted to say. She seemed so clean and pure right then. With a great body, of course. Clean and pure with a great body. And those gorgeous grey-blue eyes and wild brown hair raging round that warm open face. I wanted her but I was so scared I wanted to throw up.

'You – you're made for this,' I muttered. 'You're the kind of girl that should be with him.'

'Who?'

'Josh.'

She laughed.

'No – seriously,' I said, 'you should marry him. You're perfect. You're kind and friendly and . . . well . . . you know, good lookin' an' all . . . and I'm . . . I'm the opposite of all of that.'

She moved next to me and leant over the balustrade for a moment. She looked over at the girls on the street. They were packing up school now.

'Like them, you mean.'

'Yea, exactly. Clean, tidy, organised, willing.'

'Hey! I'm not *that* willing!'

'You know what I mean.'

She looked back at me and shook her head.

'I don't think he cares about that,' she said softly, 'I don't think he's looking for good and clean and right. That's why I sent you the story he told. Remember that? I think he's looking for someone like you, Tom. I changed the end by the way.'

I gave her a wary glance. 'The end of what?'

'The end of the story. In Josh's version the boy goes home. Has a party. A feel-good ending. Just like *Pretty Woman*. But I wasn't sure you were ready for that.'

Pretty Woman? I rolled my eyes. 'Why does every girl love Richard Gere?'

''Cause he's dangerous. Like Josh, in a way. Ahh . . . you can't beat it. I love *Pretty Woman*. The perfect Cinderella story. I love that bit when he takes the necklace to the manager and the manager looks at it and talks about how it must be hard to part with something so precious. That sublime feel-good ending.'

'I prefer *About a Boy* when Hugh Grant says he's an island – he's Ibiza and everyone else can get stuffed.'

'Ah – but he changes, and that has a feel-good ending too.'

I scowled and moved away from her and found myself staring at a huge green lizard inching along the wall towards an unsuspecting gecko.

'D'you think Loung Ung got a feel-good ending?' I said.

She glanced at her book and shook her head.

'Course not. Life's too . . . harsh, too untidy. But it doesn't stop you hoping, does it? I'll keep watching *Pretty Woman* and I'll keep reading *First They Killed My Father* – that's the whole picture. That's life. Hopefully there will be a feel-good ending one day, somewhere out there at the end of everything, there has to be . . . In the meantime, we live with the struggles – we live with each other.' She slipped a glance towards me, fixing me with those searching grey-blue eyes. 'I'm scared, Tom. I pretend I'm not, but I am.'

'What? I thought you said you weren't scared! I'm the coward, remember? You're sorted.'

She laughed. 'No, I'm not. We're both sick and we both need a doctor, and maybe we'll always be sick. But while we're limping along we can – what did he say – be a web page for people. For each other.'

She went quiet. I wanted to kiss her but I think that would have missed the point and probably earned me a slap. I tried to do the right thing, I tried to think about higher things like being sick and needing doctors and limping along and web pages – but I couldn't help it. I still wanted to snog her. She was perfect – everything I wanted right then. And that was on a day when I'd stood in a place where twenty thousand had been tortured to death, and then I'd sunbathed in a mass grave.

I still just wanted to kiss her. It was all I could think about.

You see, it was true – I really never was gonna be as good as her. I was never gonna be what Josh wanted.

Sixth Bit

Anaesthetic

Before we knew it, it was six o'clock and the darkness was already washing over the Cambodian streets. Sal ran off to get changed and I went in search of more beers to stock the mini bar.

I found myself in the hotel foyer and, for a moment, I wandered outside. The hot air hit me like a blast furnace but I stayed to soak up something of the night. I strolled down to the street beyond the hotel gates and looked out on the Asian night. Cicadas and crickets knocked out a scratch symphony and chimes still jangled above the noise of the traffic.

Lamps and fires blazed beside the road. Here and there curled bodies dozed on slatted counters while whole families gathered around on others, hungry for their late meal. The sounds and smells of the cooking filled the hot evening air. And on the back of the speeding mopeds young women, ornately dressed, perched side-saddle on their way to somewhere.

'Another world, isn't it?'

I started. It was Jude.

'Be careful with her,' he said. 'Don't get distracted.'

I blinked.

'What?'

'She's a nice girl but remember what we're doing here.'

I asked him what the hell he was talking about. As far as I knew the only thing I was doing here was waiting to get back home.

He nodded then said, 'Don't con yourself, Tom. Today affected you. And if not you, I know it affected some of the others. I told you, things are changing.'

And he melted back into the darkness, the way he always managed to melt away into the darkness after our little chats, it was like he only existed to pop up every so often and spook me.

I was about to melt away myself when I spotted Josh crossing the shadowed street outside. He'd had a haircut.

'Where d'you get that?' I asked.

He grinned. 'Just round the corner, there's a blind guy who cuts hair on the street.'

'What?'

'Yea, I did him a deal, he cut my hair and . . . well, I . . . I gave him . . . I made some mud and . . .'

He seemed suddenly embarrassed.

'You made some mud?'

'Yea, I took some of the red dust, you know, like this stuff here, and mixed it with spit and smeared it on . . .'

'On what?'

'On his eyes.'

'You did what?'

Josh sighed and shook his head.

'You're never there to see it, Tom. That's your trouble. It's like you always miss the key moments.'

'So what did I miss?'

'You should have been there. It doesn't matter.'

'When do we go home?' I snapped.

'We're just getting started, mate,' he said.

I turned and jabbed him in the chest.

'No,' I yelled, the anger and confusion suddenly rising in my voice, 'you're the one just getting started. You've got your own little show here and you're having a ball. But for the rest of us it's weird. We haven't got a clue what's going on. You drag us out here, tell us it's got something to do with God, then you weep like a big girl over some genocide . . . Just tell us. What's going on? What do you want from us?'

He stared at me, and the staring went on for a long time. In the end I wanted to flinch and run and hide in a cupboard somewhere but I wouldn't, I wanted an answer. Eventually he gave me one, or rather, he gave me another question.

'The real question is, what do you want from me, Tom?'

'Typical politician,' I said, 'answer a question with a question.'

I turned to leave but he pulled me back.

'I'm serious, Tom. If you don't answer the question, I can't answer it for you. What do you want from me?'

'Seriously?'

He nodded.

'One of two things – either that it was like I never met you and none of this shite happened. Or, that I start to feel good about myself and feel like I want to do things other than drink and stare at naked women.'

He frowned. 'You want to lose your sex drive?'

'No! No! But I don't want it to feel like a cage. Sheesh, what am I doing? I don't want you knowing all this.'

'Then keep your voice down, cause I won't be the only one.'

In the street nearby, families were taking a break from their bowls of fish and rice to stop and watch the free show.

'Maybe Sal can help you with all that,' he said.

I turned on him, eyes blazing.

'What does that mean?'

'You're lonely, Tom. And sex should be more than an anaesthetic for the past.' He jabbed a fierce finger in my chest, yet even as he did it he was smiling. 'Take a risk,' he said.

I backed off.

'I already did take a risk,' I told him, 'I got on a plane and came with you to Cambodia.'

And I walked away, my cheeks burning and my head pounding.

Max Bygraves

I spent the evening in a dark mood. My head a place of corridors filled with dark figures waiting to pounce. Josh took us to a restaurant on the outskirts of Phnom Penh – I've no idea how he knew all these places, he just did. We passed miles of eating-houses and eventually we pulled up outside the door of an impressive white stone building. Six Cambodian women greeted us with the kind of smiles designed to warm our hearts and stir our loins. They bowed, showed us to our seats and plied us with beer. I was so out of it I didn't even realise Sal was perched next to me. Most times I can't see a good thing till it waves me goodbye. Why should she care about me anyway, some skinny Jeremy Clarkson look-alike, with rampant hair, wide eyes and little fashion sense? Pick the next guy wandering round the corner and he'd have a shed-load more wit and charm than this loser.

We ordered piles of Chinese food and it came in a random order, side dishes, starters, main courses, soups, salads – it all arrived like traffic bunching at a round-about.

'I want to tell you a story,' Josh said.

'Oh great – he's Max Bygraves now,' said Jimmy, but his brother was strangely quiet.

'In fact,' he went on, 'I think tonight is a good night for stories.'

Some of the girls looked at him and nodded. Most of the lads kept their heads down and tore into the food. Sal offered me a bowl of rice. I forced a smile. She could see it was forced and pushed the corners of my mouth down with her fingers.

'Oi! Listen to the story,' Josh said.

The others looked at us and I suddenly filled up with an uncanny mixture of embarrassment and pride. This girl, at least for now, at least in this place, at least before I somehow blew it, was with me.

'If you build a house out of cards it'll collapse, or let's say . . . if you build a castle in a swamp it'll sink without trace. Let's bring it up to date – if you load your computer with virus-infected software, then it'll implode. So instead we protect ourselves, we do all we can to avoid that. So why do we so quickly construct our lives on dodgy, virus-infected material?'

A dozen shoulders shrugged. No one was in the mood for risking wrong answers. Josh glanced at Jack and Jimmy.

'Or take sea and sand. Good for surfing, bad for building. I mean – you wouldn't surf over rocks, now, would you? But rocks are great if you're building. Sometimes it seems as if we get it the wrong way round. We surf over boulders and build on sand.'

He looked for a response but we were just shovelling rice. So he waited and watched us shifting handfuls of white and yellow food for a while, then he said, 'What about this? You plant rice in flooded fields. The wetter the better. Right? (Pause) I'll take that as a yes. OK, so there's this rice farmer, he goes out one day and instead of carefully planting in the flooded fertile fields he takes huge great handfuls of the stuff and just throws it everywhere. On the roads, in the hills, in the car parks, in the rubbish tips, in the brothels, in the restaurants, in the bars, on the airport runway. He just walks around chucking these precious rice shoots all around. And everywhere he goes there are random patches of wet ground in unexpected places. And so some of the shoots take root and start growing. Perhaps a quarter of what he sows. Now that's dodgy farming. Ask any rice farmer. You don't go wasting your rice on dusty roads and filthy rubbish heaps. You sow all your shoots in wet ground so you get the best return. Not this farmer, he sows everywhere, in the hope that in the most unexpected places, rice will grow and the seed will bear fruit.'

A grinning, yellow-toothed businessman leant over from a nearby table.

'Bad farmer,' he said, tapping the table with a nicotine-stained finger, 'bad farmer.'

Josh laughed. 'No,' he said, 'generous farmer. When you own all the shoots, you can afford to be liberal.'

The businessman laughed too, but he carried on muttering about bad farming as he returned to his own mountain of food.

'So what do you guys think? Bad farming?'

'I'm not a farmer,' said Andy.

'No,' said Josh, 'but you are a free-thinking individual. What do you think? What's it mean?'

Andy swigged some of his beer and thought for a while. Then he jabbed a finger at Josh and said confidently, 'No idea.'

Josh laughed again. 'How can I make you see it? The world's littered with signs and stories about God. Why won't you open your eyes? Look for signs of life. All right. Listen up, I'll say this only once. The rice shoots are like the signs of God, and God is generous, so he takes risks and scatters them everywhere. Some of the ground is concrete, like car parks or runways; that represents the people whose eyes are too blind, whose hearts too hard to receive anything and before you know it, those shoots are gone. Some of the ground is like rubbish tips and scree slopes; that represents those whose lives have enough substance to start the shoot growing, but not enough to make it last. At the first sign of struggle or heartache the new growth dies.'

Why did he look at me at that moment?

'Some of the ground is like rough hillside, or roadside soil. Some people are receptive enough for the seed to start growing in their life, but not enough to help it flourish. It takes root and it bears fruit, but it never matures properly. Hmmm . . .' he nodded, 'I think a lot of shoots land in that kind of soil. And sometimes that kind of ground is mistaken for good ground. But the good ground, the wet, flooded soil, that's tucked away in all kinds of places, often unexpected places. A window box here, a flooded garden there. An old derelict swimming pool, a forgotten pond, an abandoned bathtub, a rotting car, a discarded washing machine. Good soil is everywhere, and the shoots spring up in the unlikely places, bearing all kinds of fruit. Now, there are people like that all over the place.'

He paused and pondered his next move; there was less eating going on now and a lot more staring.

'You know, it's very difficult for religious people to really get God. It's hard for them to grasp the one they talk about all the time. In fact, there's more chance that

Jo Brand would win Miss Universe. They say so many of the right things, and have all the right ideas. But that can be just the thing that puts a gulf between them and the kingdom of heaven. There was a vineyard back in England, and every day a woman called Gina visited it and picked the grapes. She had no idea who the owner was and had never met him, but she loved picking grapes and she made fantastic wine. She was allowed to go in because two generations back her family had been given the freedom of the vineyard – they could go in anytime and just help themselves. Now, living in that vineyard was a young guy called Mick. He knew the owner very well and spent all of his time in the vineyard. He was a poet and wrote a lot about the beauty of the land and the bountiful crops of grapes. But he never made any wine. The vineyard was massive, but one day Gina came across Mick's little house as she was picking grapes, and Mick came out and saw her, and he was well miffed to find this unknown girl picking the fruit.

'"Stop it!" he shouted. "Those grapes don't belong to you."

'Gina was frightened and went home confused.

'The next day Mick went and reported the thief to the owner.

'But the owner was angry.

'"She makes the best wine," he said. "You don't make any. You celebrate the vineyard and you speak about me, and you write about the good things there. But you never pick grapes and you never make wine. Which of you is doing the right thing?"

'Mick was afraid of the answer so he said he didn't know. So the owner encouraged him to go home and think about it. So Mick did, and he wrote an amazing poem about his conversation with the owner and his meeting with Gina. But he still didn't make any wine.

Meanwhile Gina moved away. She found an olive grove, bought a share of it with the money she'd saved from making wine and started producing olive oil. People live what they believe, even if they don't intend to – they can't help it. Their faith oozes out of their lives. But sometimes, the beliefs they show are very different to the beliefs they claim. Don't be deceived into thinking that you must join the ranks of those who say the right words. Just keep on picking grapes and making wine, and if you've never yet tried it – have a go.'

Deathly orange blood

We left the hotel at seven-thirty the next morning for the flight at nine. We were going north, where the Khmer Rouge were still causing trouble – what do they call them – pockets of resistance. We flew over the great lake, Tonle Sap, aboard an old propeller-driven plane and felt every air pocket, every breath of turbulence, and when we finally touched down, the ground felt like a waterbed for a while. We stumbled out into the floodlit day and mooched around drinking water in the terminal. Jack kept checking his boot and I figured he'd got Nat's shooter somewhere down there. He and Jimmy spent most of the time scowling, Si too, but they were less vocal and I had the feeling something was going on. I think Josh was working hard to rebuild the friendship with them.

We left the airport and Andy and Nat and a couple of the girls kicked a deflated ball around while we waited for Josh to fix transport. He hired a few cyclos, bike taxis pedalled by wafer-thin couriers who took your money with a ready smile and looked as if they could make those wheels go round forever. As we left the airport in convoy, three of us jammed on each cyclo, we passed a family of five, and fifteen chickens all aboard a single vehicle.

'We'll go to the hotel and then head up to Angkor Wat for sundown,' Josh called as we drew alongside at a junction. Then he took a long look at me and added, 'Keep drinking lots, Tom, you're looking a bit side-whacked, mate. Don't get dehydrated. Here.' He threw me a fresh bottle of water. 'Don't want you pegging out before we've finished this.'

Finished what? Too late, the cyclo driver hit the pedal and Josh was gone.

We ended up at the Salida hotel – a no-nonsense paradise for jet-lagged pilgrims. It was a newly built four-star hotel surrounded by palms and ornate gardens, hidden well back from the road in its own tropical grounds. We checked in, dumped our bags and made straight for the temples. As we neared Angkor Wat the mighty sun was just beginning its descent. We made it just in time cause when that sun goes, it really goes. It was dropping like a recoiling beast, mortally wounded and shedding its deathly orange blood across the ancient stone. The three towers of the Wat rose like mighty fir cones from the ancient walls, the whole place basking in the auburn glow; below the towers the symmetrical complex sprawled in a jigsaw of colonnades, corbel roofs and decorated stonework. I could tell you it was mind-blowing, but what's the point? Those few words wouldn't blow your mind.

'Man, that's awesome,' said Nat, and he meant it.

We stood and nodded. Sal appeared beside me and caught her breath. She caught my arm too which was, of course, the best bit.

'A thousand years, guys,' Josh mused, 'a thousand years this place has stood and absorbed the life of the

Khmer people. Every pulse, every heartbeat for a millennium. What must that be like? Kind of steeps the place in a time zone all of its own, doesn't it?'

We nodded sagely though we weren't that bothered about the question. Beer, food, girls and then maybe every heartbeat of the last millennium, that was more like our agenda. But no one said that; in the presence of religious greatness you can't be so earthy – you can't let reality leak out all over divine things, now, can you?

Josh walked ahead in silence. I found myself catching him up ahead of the group.

'You know, I'm starving and I could murder a beer,' he said, and I didn't know what to say to that. 'Sal's beautiful, isn't she? And she's onto you, mate. I can see that. Anyone can. She's a great girl. Don't mess it up. Tom, you can jack in uni and drink away your benefit but don't waste this kind of chance. You see, mate, she's stunning on the inside too,' he jabbed my chest, 'where it counts.'

Again I said nothing.

We passed a trio of musicians, all of them amputees, playing a repetitive, tuneless medley on pan pipes and drums. Josh tossed a note into a coloured hat beside the single foot of the drummer. A dozen children spotted the gesture and herded around him. Jimmy and Jack came from nowhere and shooed them away, though it took some doing.

'Wow! Wow!' Josh was right there, trying to stop the shooing. 'Don't do that!' he said, but by then the kids had latched onto Miz and the other girls. Miz seemed to be a magnet for them and spent most of her time in those temples surrounded by street children.

Now that I stopped to look I realised the place was awash with beggars – a meandering crocodile of children and amputees snaking along the pathways and between the buildings. Once you saw past the splendour of the temples then you started to glimpse the crippled community living in the cracks.

'This is the real splendour of the place, the real time-less beauty,' Josh said.

'What's so great about starving kids and crawling men?' I muttered.

'You'll see,' he said. Then he stopped. 'I think I'll make sure I'm here at dawn tomorrow for the sunrise. Wanna come?'

I shrugged.

'Well, I'll bring Jack and Jimmy and Si. They could do with a shot in the arm.'

He shut up then and we turned and looked back for the others. Jack and Miz were sparring with each other; Miz always gave as good as she got. She was as cool as Jack any day and was never gonna be outsmarted by him. Andy and Nat meanwhile were chatting up two of the other girls. Matt was poring over a guide book spouting facts about twelfth-century Khmer masonry. Lines of candles adorned balustrades, lit by the travellers and pilgrims that ventured behind us. The scent of incense filled the air, rising from the long smoking spindles dotted along the parapets in between the low glimmering lights. It was like a restaurant on Valentine's night – and when I spotted Sal she was walking far too closely to Si, slipping her arm through his.

Ghosts at dawn

We arranged to meet Josh at eight the next morning. He took Si and the twins with him at dawn but the rest of us lay in, ate platefuls of eggs and fruit and went on later. When we got to the Wat I kicked myself for turning down his invitation.

Jack and Si were at the base of the final climb to the top of the Wat. They were unusually wide-eyed and the scowls that had taken up residence had clearly left town. Jack looked almost in shock.

'What happened up there?' Miz asked, as we crowded round them.

Jack shook his head. 'Later,' he said. 'It was awesome but I can't say now.'

'Why not? Tell me.' She punched him on the shoulder but he shook his head.

'Not now, Miz,' he said, and he got up and walked away.

Jimmy crouched in a sullen trance as he sat at the base of the craggy narrow steps that led to the pinnacle of the temple.

'The National Trust would have a field day with this lot,' I said, perching next to him.

The final set of steps was steep, slippery and catastrophically uneven. Like a mountain of fat pitta breads, piled precariously on top of each other.

'They'd have installed a Stannah stairlift by now,' I said.

Jimmy wagged a thumb over his shoulder at the steps. 'Up there, you should have been there, man, you missed something.'

Again! I missed it again. I was consistent if nothing else.

'What happened?'

'I'm not sure. Ghostly figures. Dry ice. Floodlights. A voice in the sky.'

I glanced up at the top; if there'd been a close encounter up there it was long gone now.

'Could have been the monks having some kind of service.'

He laughed. 'Yea, right,' he said, 'and I'm Britney Spears.' Then he frowned. 'There's more to Josh than meets the eye, you know – trouble is, having seen it, you can't pretend you didn't.' He put a hand on my shoulder. He seemed unusually restrained, gentle even. 'Maybe you were better not to come. You don't have the snag of having to choose.'

And he got up and walked away. A tumble of little rocks passed me by and I turned to see Josh.

He was just coming down the steps from the Wat, and even as he did a crowd of beggars moved in towards us. They chatted in Khmer and waved a variety of begging bowls and calloused hands and we were soon surrounded.

He fired a quick glance at me and said, 'I wish you'd believe without seeing this, Tom, but if it helps, here it is.'

He waded into the crowd and knelt at the foot of a man on crutches. I lost sight of him for a moment, but when he stood up he was holding a crutch in his hand. I half expected the beggar to keel over, but instead the guy yelled something that was halfway between a sob and a scream and then he started kicking up red dust with his feet. In an instant, a dozen amputees were clawing at Josh. He was buried alive in the bodies. There was more yelling, more dust, and before you could say Casualty half a dozen people were stamping the ground and punching the air with new bits of their body. I stared. I couldn't quite piece it together in my mind. The impossible was happening, but it just looked so manufactured. Like it was CGI or something. Josh was in a movie and the special effects guys had really done their homework. It all looked so convincing it had to be made up. It went on and on and on. Broken bodies turning into re-rendered people, Josh pulling arms and legs out of thin air like some conjurer in a prosthetics lab.

Meeting people and pedalling magic

'Who touched me?'

Josh swung around and kept spinning on the spot, clouds of dust kicking up at his feet. 'Somebody touched me. I felt the power suck out of me.'

'They're all touching you,' I said.

'No, this was different. Someone pinched a miracle. Hun, Hun,' he beckoned to our driver. 'Come here, ask them who touched me.'

The crowd was growing by the second now, over a hundred of them; people were laughing and yelling in Khmer. The noise was deafening.

Hun mounted the steps and screamed at them. They all stopped and froze. Then a hundred hands went up. All the kids yelling 'Me, me!' in Khmer.

'Oh, this is hopeless,' Si said.

'No, it's not. Ask again, Hun.'

Again he screamed and again everyone froze and again all the kids stuck their hands up and yelled back. Then I spotted him, at the edge, just escaping the crush of the crowd. A little old wizened monk in his dirty saffron robe, hunched and shuffling along, most of his weight on a stick almost as bent as he was. Josh spotted him too, and he quickly ran over and took the guy to one side. The monk's eyes were like two dark saucers sunk into his skull and his mouth was a toothless circle. But as Josh whispered to him his face cracked into a gummy smile, the years fell away from his face and his body unfolded until he no longer needed the stick. How they communicated was a mystery. But the old guy stood up straight and went away with a sudden spring in his step. Something had happened, but once again I wasn't in on it. No one was, just Josh and the toothless monk.

'I came to meet people – not pedal magic,' Josh shouted at us. 'Come on, let's get out of here.'

Getting back to the buses was a tough one. The paths were lined with busking beggars and souvenir-selling children; add to that the throng that was still following us, most of them with new body parts to exercise, and you can imagine it was like rush hour on the underground. Myself, I was in some kind of daze. You know how you always want to see a miracle and imagine that it'll somehow disperse every single one of your doubts and show you the meaning of life forever? Well, it doesn't. Or at least it wasn't like that for me. I'd just seen a dozen miracles. Twenty, thirty. Yet, somehow I could find reasons to explain every one of them. Not cause I wanted to. I just have this instinct, this gift for not believing my very own eyes.

Arm-in-arm with Si

Back at the Salida, I sat in the bar alone for a long time, nursing my beer and seeing the faces of a hundred amputees reflected in it. In my head, Sal came and joined me and we talked it all out and I became a believer and we had great sex and got married. All in the time that it takes to drink two bottles of Angkor beer. But not in reality. In reality there was no sign of Sal, and I was left with my doubts and the last vision I'd had of her walking away arm-in-arm with big Si.

I fell asleep at the bar. When I woke it was two in the morning and Jude was sitting next to me in the half light.

I saw him and nearly fell off my stool.

'Is it starting to make sense?' he said.

'At this time in the morning? Nothing makes sense, mate.'

'You wait till we get back home. News will spread, things will happen. Have another beer.' He shoved a glass over to me. I looked at it.

'You're right,' I said. 'Things are changing. I don't want any more beer right now.'

I started to walk away.

'I see you took my advice about the girl,' he called as I went.

I stopped. 'What did you say?'

'I see you gave up on the girl.' He raised his glass and winked as he drank it down.

I don't know where the energy came from, or the power, or the ability. I've never punched anyone in my life before. But something came from somewhere. I lunged at him, swung hard and smacked his jaw, pummelling his glass right out of his hands. As I heard the smash I lunged again, this time catching him on the temple. As I swung a third time he was ready and his left hand grabbed my flailing fist. I could feel the knuckles crunch inside his iron fingers.

'Save your energy,' he said, blood oozing from the corner of his mouth. 'You'll have plenty of fighting to do when we get home.'

'Don't . . . don't . . .' I wanted to say something cool, something to shut him up, something to hurt him, but nothing would come. 'Just shut up about Sal,' was all I could manage.

And I went to bed, my fist throbbing in time with my heartbeat.

Self-conscious and a little bit drunk

We made one more trip to the temples. We went the next morning while it was still relatively quiet. The hippies and the tourists were still tucked up, probably with each other. We trawled around Angkor Thom, the old capital of Angkor, and stopped in the centre to stare up at the Bayon faces. Four enormous carved heads of the king who built his own monument.

'They reckon the whole of ancient Rome could fit inside this complex,' Matt said. 'It was rediscovered in 1912 by some French dude who got the shock of his life when he stumbled out of the jungle and bumped into this lot. Them faces are called the smile of Angkor. There's over two hundred of them round here.'

We did our best to look unimpressed.

'You have a history book for breakfast, then, did you?' said Nat.

'I'm just saying,' said Matt.

The lads took to clambering over the crumbling walls and tiled roofs, while Miz and Sal and their mates shot posy photos amongst the giant roots of the trees that protruded from the building tops.

'*Tomb Raider* was made here, dudes,' said Nat as he straddled eight hundred years of brickwork. 'You see – I know history, too.'

Half an hour later we stood below the mighty walls of Angkor Wat one last time, water buffalo basking in the river behind us, while Josh, in a strange pensive mood, ran his fingers over the ancient stone.

'We should go,' said Si, 'the locals'll be back and you'll never get away.'

'You know,' said Josh, 'as awesome as all this is, one day it'll be gone. Nothing lasts forever. And these walls prove it. Look, they've been crumbling for centuries. One day, this'll be pure jungle again.'

'So?' asked Nat.

'So what does last forever? What can be rebuilt and never destroyed?'

'What are you talking about?' asked Si.

Then a still small voice answered.

'Lives. People. They last forever.'

We all turned and looked towards the quiet reply. It was Sal.

Josh smiled at her and nodded. 'People,' he said, 'we spend so much time worrying about things, we insure them, we repair them, we replace them. But Sal – you can never be replaced. Jack can't be, Miz can't be, not even Tom and all his questions. Irreplaceable. Stuff dies, it rots, it withers, and though it sometimes takes centuries – it crumbles. So I say it's better to invest in the stuff that will last forever. This temple . . .' he jabbed his own chest with his thumb, 'this temple will last forever, and even though you may see it fall, don't believe your eyes. When this temple gets knocked down, it'll get up again.'

Sal waited as the others walked away. I was waiting, too, but not for her. I was waiting so I could walk on my own. She was having none of it.

'Enjoy your drink?' she asked.

'What?'

'I saw you at the bar last night with Jude. I couldn't sleep. I came looking for you.'

I stared at her. 'You're kidding me.'

She laughed at my expression. 'No, believe it or not I was . . .' She looked down. 'I was lonely.'

We started to walk.

'Did you have a good time with Jude?' she asked. 'No one else ever seems to talk to him. He freaks me.'

'I hit him.'

'What?' It was her turn to stare. 'Why?'

Oh great – where d'you begin with a story like that?

'I was jealous,' I said, and I left it at that.

She slipped her arm in mine and I immediately felt self-conscious and a little bit drunk.

Hun

Sal was still beside me as we slipped into a cyclo and made for the airport. Hun came along to guide us back to the airport; he sat up front and chatted to the impassive driver. The wide streets were lined with bottle stalls and food stands, selling fruit, water, beer, Coke, Fanta, fish and meat. The flies were prevalent and the heat as ever bore down with a vengeance. Hun stopped at a stall and bought a large unripened coconut.

'The milk is good, you should drink,' he said seriously.

The girl behind the stall was in her late teens, she had beautiful almond eyes and soft, open features so typical of the women there. She took a hatchet and hacked swiftly across the ends of the bright green fruit. With a few lightning strokes she'd shaped the bottom and hewed off the top. She pulled a plastic straw from a jug and threaded it through the narrow hole at the apex.

'Taste it, is good,' said Hun, as the girl passed it over, and she started on another as I handed it to Sal.

She took it and winked as she drew on the straw.

Hun handed me a second and I took a mouthful of the juice. It was grainy, sweet and tangy. We bought a few more and gave the girl a faltering Khmer thank-you. Hun placed his hands together in the typical Khmer greeting. He bowed a little and hopped back on board.

As we rode on, I tapped Hun on the shoulder.

'Were you here in Cambodia when the Khmer Rouge came, Hun? In the seventies, wasn't it?'

'In the time of Pol Pot?' Hun's face grew sombre. 'Yes, I was here when soldiers came. I remember tanks rolling past our house, people cheering. Very bad time.'

'How old were you?'

'Me, I was . . . seven. Yes, seven.'

'Can you tell me about it? Please?'

A weariness settled on the Cambodian; a resigned, distant sadness fell upon his soft features.

'Yes, I can tell you about it. Soldiers came and they told us to leave, to go for three days and then we come back. They marched us out of the capital, me, my brothers, my sisters, all my family. We walk for long time, out, out, away from the city, out into the country. Many people go with us. Some people die, can't make it. The soldiers leave them on the road. Then we came to a village, all burnt out, houses very bad. The soldiers tell us to live there. Twelve of us in a burnt house. After some time they come back and take my uncle, I followed them into the forest . . . they killed him. Hit him. Like this.' He motioned with his fists. 'Then we get very hungry, no food. Soldiers bring us nothing. They make us work in the fields, but they give us nothing. And no cooking, no one is allowed to cook. Very dangerous. If they do the soldiers come and shoot them. One family tried, the soldiers see the smoke and they come and kill them. So me and my sister, Song, we run off into the forest to get food. We eat bugs and butterflies, and roots. We eat all things to stay alive. I remember one day I was with my sister and she find some food, some rice in a bag, she stole four maybe five grains. Then we see a soldier, he come running and she panic. What to do with the rice? So I take the grains from her and put them inside my hat. Like this.'

He took off his baseball cap and mimed the action.

'Then I put it back on and when the soldier come he tell me to take off my hat. I did and he sees the rice. So he took me out to the road and took a piece of the fence and the wire by the road, and he hit me with it, many times.'

Again Hun mimed the action.

'Many times.'

The Cambodian swallowed and cleared his throat noisily as tears welled in his eyes.

'Many times.'

'How many of your family survived, Hun? How many lived through it?'

'Through the famine? Er, just me and my sister. Everyone else died, my uncles, my aunts, my cousins, my brothers, my parents. But you know, I think they were fortunate because they died of starvation, and not by the soldiers.'

He bent his head and clubbed his hand across the back of his neck.

'Not in the fields, you mean,' Sal said. 'In the Killing Fields?'

'No, not in the Killing Fields. I wish I could have helped them. I wish I could, but I couldn't. So now I help you, and Josh, and others who come, and together we help poor people, and when I do that the pain I feel here . . .' He tapped his chest, 'it goes away a little. Every night when I go to sleep I see my brothers' faces. I feel the pain. Every night I feel the pain. But it gets better, when I help other people it gets better.'

Seventh Bit

Ancient history

A week later and it was all ancient history. The heat, the temples, the cyclos, the coconuts. Gone. The onset of the English summer had stalled for a while and the streets of Cornwall were like the skies, grey and dull. No more red dirt or jack fruit, no more Phnom Penh or big adventure. It all seemed like a dream. No more Sal either. She didn't call and I, as usual, had no back-up plan. I didn't know her number. I didn't even know her surname.

So I started digging up my own past. As sometimes happens when you've made a fracture in your life, I found an appetite for other things. I went to the old family home and dug out old boxes of books and photos in the loft, air pistols and Action Men I'd had as a kid. More old records and a couple of fishing rods. A toolbox full of hooks and flies and nylon thread took me right back. I'd had good times messing about by the river.

I spent a while messing about again, catching nothing but trying all the same. I wanted to savour Cambodia, frame it forever in my head – even though I'd spent much of the time there waiting for the plane home, now it was gone I wanted it back. I was desperate to break out of my life here, the endless cycle of drink and TV. Sitting by the river for long hours was soothing and distracting, and it gave me ideas. I thought on some of the things Josh had said and I replayed the punch I'd lan-ded on Jude again and again and again. I decided I'd find out where Sal lived. If she was lonely enough to come looking for me at night, then I was lonely enough to go searching for her in the day. I went to the place where I knew I could find one of the lads. I went to the pub.

The pact

I found Josh sitting in the Greyhound. The place was quiet and, unusually, he was sitting alone.

'He's dead, Tom,' was all he said as soon as I sat down.

'Who?'

'John. I just heard the news. They killed him.'

'Who did?'

'I'm scared, Tom. I see where this is going and I'm scared.'

'Why? You'll be all right. You've done nothing wrong.'

'Neither had John.' He took a sup of his pint and offered to buy me one. 'I feel so alone sometimes, Tom, usually when I'm not alone. I take a lot of time out, go and walk, shout at the sky at night, whisper some prayers at daybreak. Mostly I sit and soak up what's around me. So much of God in this world, Tom, so much of him. But when I'm with people, and they just want to argue, or fight back or prove a point, or just look better than other people – then I feel empty. I feel as if I'm failing. As if no one will ever get it. Even John didn't always see it. Remember that time he sent some mates to check me out? He should have known, should have remembered . . .'

We'd been in the Greyhound one night, when a gang of John's mates had burst in and come straight over.

'What's going on?' one of them said, a tall guy with ginger dreadlocks and a spike through his eyebrow.

Josh had grinned at him and offered his hand.

'You're one of John's friends, aren't you?' Josh had said to him. 'How is he? How's John doing? Does he need anything?'

The man hadn't smiled back. 'Yea, he needs to know why you're not doing your job.'

'What?'

'You're making him look stupid, he told everyone that change was on the way. He told people to watch you and you'd kick out the government and mobilise the people.'

'But . . . I'm not here to do that.'

'You're supposed to be turning things around. Not hanging out drinking pints and playing slot machines. What's going on? John's not sure any more, you know. He's losing faith, he's in prison on a trumped-up charge and you're out here partying. He wants to know – has he made a mistake with you?'

Josh shook his head sadly. 'He made no mistake,' he said. 'Tell him people's lives are changing, but you have to look closely. Don't judge by what's on the surface. Tell him . . . tell him that pact we made wasn't wrong . . .'

More gadgets than a Bond car

Josh looked up at me and a sudden smile sneaked across his lips.

'When I was twelve, we made a pact,' he said.

'Yea, you mentioned it once.'

'Yea, I'd been to London for the day with my parents. I loved travelling with my old man. He knows so much – about trains and history and the war. I soaked it up. He knew all the quirky little things that you never read in books.

'Well, that day I was waiting for the old guy outside of this tobacconists . . . he used to love smoking this stuff that smelt foul but apparently tasted great. He always wore the same old cardigan back then, with two little woollen pockets; he kept his tobacco pouch in one and this amazing smoker's knife in the other. It had more gadgets than a Bond car . . . Anyway, I was waiting for him when I saw these three stretch limos roll up and all these suits got out. Bodyguards everywhere. Before you knew it photographers were flashing away and reporters oozed out of the cracks in the pavement. They were all over the place. They were pumping these guys with the usual questions and suddenly I got all inspired and thought I'd have a go. So I called out a question of my own. And everything stopped. It was like they'd pressed the pause button, and then, just like a movie, they all turned to look at me in slow motion. I can't remember what the question was now, but you'd have thought I'd just disclosed who shot JFK. Then, before you know it, these people were taking an interest in me. I think they were MPs. And I just fired off these questions and when they came back at me with the usual bull I told 'em they were coming back at me with the usual bull. The reporters loved it. They couldn't get enough. A five-minute photo shoot turned into a half-hour dialogue. In the end, my old man appeared in the crowd looking all harried and stressed. He'd brought the police too. The poor guy had thought I'd been abducted. I think he grounded me for a ridiculous amount of time. I made the main News that night, and when my mum saw it she looked at the old guy and just said, "Told you so." Anyway, that was the day John and I made the pact. He'd change the world, and I'd finish it. Well, looks like it's up to me now, then.' He paused. 'Hard to lose someone you love, isn't it, Tom?' He said that last phrase in such a gentle tone that it caught me unawares. Another stray missile found its mark inside.

'Yea,' I muttered, but I didn't look him in the eye, 'it is.'

He sighed and massaged his eyes with his fingers.

'The newspapers reported John's death as another prison suicide,' he said with another sigh, 'but the word on the street is different. John didn't fall, Tom, he was pushed.'

Reality TV

At that moment, a familiar image appeared on the pub television.

'Angkor Wat!' I said, pointing at the set mounted high above the bar.

Suddenly hordes of Cambodians were crowding round the camera lens.

Josh got up and took a few steps closer. His face darkened.

'This isn't good,' he said. 'Can you turn it up, mate?'

The barman, a young guy in jeans and a Red Hot Chilli Peppers T-shirt, shrugged and hunted for the TV gun.

A single Khmer face appeared on the screen.

Josh let a smile invade his face.

'That's the barber I told you about – the one who gave me a haircut. He's a great guy.'

'Can't you find the sound, mate?' I said to the barman.

'I'm looking!' he said. 'They hide the remote so kids can't mess about with it.'

He slipped out the back and still we heard nothing. Then a very familiar face appeared on the screen.

'It's Nat!' I shouted. 'What's he doing up there?'

And suddenly the whole gang were there, Jack, Jimmy, Si, Andy, Matt, Nat, Miz, Sal, all of us, sitting on the steps of Angkor Wat, supping water and looking like any old tourists.

'All except Jude,' Josh muttered.

'What?'

He looked back at me.

'Does Jude have a camera? A video camera?'

'Probably.'

'Did you see him filming over there?'

Before I could reply, Jude himself appeared on the screen, mouthing something to the camera.

'Sound! We need sound!' Josh yelled, and he was getting agitated now.

But there was no sound. The barman mooched around searching half-heartedly, moving empty glasses and bags of peanuts around, but the programme ended and we were left staring at Richard and Judy doing their goldfish impressions.

Questions

And then I didn't see him for a week, until Jude came knocking on my door one night.

'He wants you,' he said. 'We got a meet-up, something's going down.'

He turned away to slip back into the shadows the way he always did, but I pulled him back.

'Wait a minute, Jude, look at me. It was you, wasn't it?'

'What was?'

'You told the press about Cambodia. You secretly filmed us out there. You've ruined it for him now.'

'No I haven't, you wait and see. I've just notched things up a level.' He stepped closer to me. 'This had to go national, Tom. Sometimes I think you have no idea what we're dealing with here.' He stared at me, his cold green eyes boring into me. 'Now come on.'

As we walked in awkward silence he pulled a gloved hand from his pocket and held it out to me.

'What's that?' I asked.

'A little bird told me you needed some.'

I looked at the wad of notes in his hand. The money he'd given me for the Cambodia trip had all but run out now.

'Why are you doing this?'

'So you don't have to worry. So you can concentrate on helping him.'

I hesitated, so he turned, grabbed my hand and pressed the notes into my palm.

'It's a hell of a lot,' I said.

'Then it'll keep you going for a while. Don't worry, it's legit. Now come on, Josh is waiting.'

We met him in the clearing behind the Old Mariner at sunset, just a few of us guys. I noticed Jack and Jimmy were there; in spite of their grand claims in Cambodia of giving up, they'd not yet returned to their mama's business. Josh was pensive, pacing around a lot, then Jimmy started in.

'Josh, now that you're, like, getting famous and on TV and all that, can you put in a good word for me and Jack – you know, when you're mixing it with the telly people? The high-ups, the execs. I mean, we're your mates and we need to find a good job. There's no good surfing programmes on terrestrial TV at the moment, know what I'm saying? I'm sure they could do with a couple of good-looking blond sea kings to . . .'

Before he could finish, Josh raised a hand.

'Let's go for a walk,' he said, and he led off before we could agree or argue.

He took us along the seafront and back into town. The seedy part, the red-light district round there doesn't exactly put Soho in the shade, but it has dark spots. I got really nervous when he stopped outside the sex shop.

'What are we doing here?' I muttered.

He didn't reply, just gestured with his head and took us inside. The place was dark and red bulbs glimmered above shelves piled with the kind of plastic playthings you'll never find in Toys R Us. The guy behind the counter frowned as we piled in like a bunch of guilty schoolboys, but when he saw Josh, he smiled. They nodded at each other and Josh took us to a back room. He poured coffee and whisky from hot and cold flasks. My head was spinning. What were we doing here?

'I think I've gotta keep my head down for a while,' he said. 'This TV exposure has made it impossible to go anywhere. I feel like a movie star. I can't do anything. I'm gonna hide out for a bit. But – every cloud and all that – I want you guys to carry on things for me.'

We looked at each other. What things?

'I'm serious – you guys can move around anonymously, you have the element of surprise. I suggest you go off in twos, pick some fishing villages and ask them if they've heard of me. Tell 'em I'm good news not bad, tell 'em what you've heard me say. And if you meet people who are sick, well – pray they'll get better. Try it, you got nothing to lose.'

'We got everything to lose,' said Si. 'Look, don't get me wrong. I'm not doubting you. In fact, ever since the trip I'm starting to get my head round who you are.'

'Really? Who am I, then, Si?'

Si licked his lips nervously and glanced at the others.

'Forget about the others, who am I?'

'On the telly they say you're a New Age prophet.'

Josh walked up to Si and looked up at him. Somewhere in the background a blue video was pumping out its groaning soundtrack. Josh stared the bigger man straight in the eye. Si pulled on his mug of whisky.

'What about it, Si? Who do you think I am?'

We were starting to enjoy the show now. Not least Jack and Jimmy. Only Andy was squirming for his big brother. Si shuffled his feet and cleared his throat, he scratched at the bristles on his head for a while and then finally he spoke. Quietly.

'You're the man.'

'The man?'

'Yea, you're not like anyone else. You used to be, but something's happened. Something's changed. You're alive, you're electric. You're buzzing. You're like, I dunno, Bond, Ghandi, Joe Strummer and John Lennon all rolled into one. I hear you talk and I see the stuff you do and . . . I can't argue with it. You used to live round the corner, yet . . . it's like you came from another planet. I can't explain it – but it's . . .' He shrugged. 'It's like you're something else . . . you're inspired, kind of mysterious, like you're . . . the man. The bloke I wish I was. Neo. The one.'

Josh's face cracked into a smile, he placed his hands on Si's shoulders and slapped him hard on both cheeks. A bizarre Eric Morecambe moment.

'Result!' he said.

It all seemed a bit over the top to me, to be honest.

'And you know who you are?' Josh was still asking tough questions.

Si frowned and looked like he was trying to calculate some rocket science.

'Don't bother answering, I'll tell you. You're the foundations for a new kind of society. The boots for a new body. You're the wheels on a car no one's seen before. And you're the rock for that house that ain't built on sand.'

Then Josh froze for a moment, turned away and began prowling again.

'To tell you the truth, things are gonna be tough from now on – harder by the day. This is not going to end well. At least, not at first.'

Si frowned and put a hand on Josh's chest to stop him circling.

'Nothing's going to happen to you. Don't worry about that. We're here – and you're Neo. If you're the one, nothing can hurt you – we won't let it.'

And then Si gave him a wink and a grin. Josh looked around at us. We weren't your usual bunch of minders, but at that moment I think we'd have squared up to a few bad guys.

'Listen, Si – that kind of talk is dangerous. Don't ever say to me, *If you're the one* – the last person who said that to me was the devil himself.'

Si started to protest. Josh's face turned to granite.

'Shut up! I'm as serious as a chemical weapon, Si. Don't get in my way. Believe me, this is going to be hard enough without you doing the Bruce Willis impression. Shut up and just trust me when I say this is not about fighting back. More aggression won't change the planet. Only sacrifice. Ya got me?' Pause, no answer. 'I said, ya got me?'

Si nodded. We'd none of us seen Josh like this before and, to be honest, Si could have easily decked him with one hand. But no one moved. We just waited for the storm to pass. Josh sighed, patted Si's shoulder and shivered for a moment. Then he smiled.

'OK, where was I? Oh yea, going out.'

'Do we have to?' It was Nat, and he was looking like he'd just swallowed a bag of nails. 'I mean, sounds like worst case scenario to me . . .'

'Everything's worst case scenario to you, Nat . . . Now, don't bother stocking up with provisions. People'll feed ya, and if you go hungry, well you need to lose a few pounds anyway. Travel light, accept what people offer you. Sleep under the stars if you have to – you'll see bits of the night you've been missing for a while, and studying the size of the universe'll remind you of the generosity of the Creator. Oh, and whatever you do – Jack,' he pointed at Jack and snapped his fingers, 'don't take that revolver.'

'I don't have a revolver,' Jack said.

'I know you got a gun, it used to be Nat's and you keep it in your boot.'

But Jack shook his head. Josh narrowed his eyes. He bent down and hitched up the leg on Jack's jeans. There was no gun.

'I did have it – but it got nicked on the trip.'

Nat's mouth fell open. 'You lost it?' he shrieked. 'Dude! That was mine!'

And he leapt at Jack and slammed him against a table. Whisky slopped all over them as they fell and rolled on the stained carpet like a couple of dogs, Nat yelling at the top of his voice. Eventually Si and Jimmy pulled them apart.

'And don't kill each other out there,' Josh said as he helped Nat up. 'You need each other. I'm not asking you to like each other. But watch each other's backs. Oh, and don't sleep around. This isn't about women and beer – think with your grey matter, not your groins.'

'It'll all go wrong,' I blurted out. I couldn't see it working at all.

'Yep,' he said, 'it may do. But some of it'll go right. Off you go, then, I'll see you back here in a fortnight. Midday two weeks from now. Go! Oh, and Tom . . .'

He handed me a beer mat from the Greyhound.

'For when you get back, motivation to return alive.'

It was a phone number.

'It's Sal's,' he said, 'thought you might need it.'

Two weeks of misery

So what can I tell you about our Cornish road trip? It wasn't Cambodia, for one thing. There were no cyclos, coconut stalls or five-star hotels and the people over here are hard. Not unfriendly, but they have a lot to lose. Especially in villages, where everyone knows every-thing about everybody. Every single day I wished I was back in Angkor, with those yelling kids and those legless soldiers. By the time Josh'd finished doing the business with the folk at the temples there must have been a thou-sand Cambodians round him. And that was in just half an hour. Over here we were lucky to get a couple of pen-sioners and a dog. As we set out from the sex shop, Andy came looking for me – he's the saint of lost causes, you know. We teamed up, found a map and set off. Thankfully, he did most of the talking. I knocked on the doors, he smiled at whoever answered. So little seemed to happen. I wanted legs growing back and blind bar-bers seeing. But all the hairdressers round there had 20/20 vision and the homeless were selling *The Big Issue*. If nothing else, I bought a lot of copies. I salved my con-science that way. We knocked on doors and asked if they'd seen Josh on the telly. Some had. A lot had for-gotten. They didn't even know where Cambodia was. The best time we had was on the last night. I was glad it was coming to an end and was all for giving up and sleeping rough in a kids' playground. But Andy spotted some hippies down by the jetty. One of them was twanging a guitar and they were inhaling something that didn't have 'Smoking Kills' on the packet.

That night made up for the rest of the time. They knew about Josh cause a local paper had run the story. One of the guys had even cut it out. We told 'em about Angkor and some of them were well impressed. They wanted to go there. We laughed and joked about anything and everything with them. We talked about Josh for a while and they listened; then one of the girls started coughing. She said she had some lung problem. I looked at Andy and Andy gave a nod. I wanted him to do the business, but he was having none of it.

It was up to me, my big chance. All I had to do was offer to say a prayer. How difficult could it be?

'Can we, like, er . . . I mean . . . we sometimes say a . . .' I couldn't get the word out. 'Well, you know, when you need something you don't have . . . you see, we think that sometimes it's worth saying a . . . sort of . . . like, a . . .'

They were looking at me as if I was the one needing divine help. Any minute now they'd offer to say one for me. Then Andy stepped in.

'Let's pray for you,' he said, and he pointed at the girl's boyfriend.

'Stick a hand on her shoulder,' Andy said, and without looking to see the result, he shut his eyes and prayed the simplest prayer in the world.

The girl stopped coughing. Don't know for how long. Certainly for the rest of that night. The gang drifted off around two in the morning, and when they went, all six of them gave us a hug. It was acutely embarrassing, but the kind of embarrassment that warmed your heart. We sat on the jetty for a long while after and said a few more prayers for them. Andy could remember their names, I didn't have a clue – I had to describe them by the length and colour of their hair. But that was all right because they all had weird hair anyway. It felt good to sit and pray for them. I don't know where those guys are now – but they made my fortnight.

When we got back the next day, Jack and Jimmy and Si assaulted us with searing tales of miracles and strange doings, converting local criminals and praying for people and seeing them walk afterwards. In my cynicism, I asked whether they could walk before the praying. Their success made me want to render Jack and Jimmy immobile for a while. It was like they'd been on another planet to me and Andy. I'd expected them just to get into fights and pick up girls, but no, they'd been to the far side and back. Jude was right about those guys – Cambodia did change things. Whatever was going on, there was no going back.

Eighth Bit

Adam Clarke and the PM

As we sat in the clearing that night, Josh looked tired but chuffed. He loved what was happening to us. He could see it in our eyes that the world was shifting.

'While you were away,' he said, when we'd all finished our tales of the unexpected, 'I slept under the night skies, and one time I saw this incredible power display. Like lightning strikes at war with thunderbolts. The whole sky was shot through with cosmic battling – infused with this electric war in heaven. It was amazing. It went on for hours. And at the finish, I saw the bad guys – you know death, disease, destruction – boom! – all blown apart.'

Jude and Jimmy loved this but it left the rest of us nodding in a kind of confused state. Then he said something that was a lot more down to earth.

'I've been invited to go on the Adam Clarke show.'

We sat up then.

'Wow! Do it!'

'I'm not sure,' he said, 'the media are sharks. It may not help at all.'

A week later we sat in the Greyhound and tuned in to see the local hero sit down with the flavour of the month. Adam Clarke walked in, boots gleaming and suit crinkle-free. After a few jokes he introduced Josh, who walked in looking like he'd just been out the back cleaning Adam's boots and pressing his suit. Josh took a seat and a nervous sip of water and the fray began.

Adam: So, Josh. Let's not mess about – are you gonna stop global warming?

Josh: (laughing) Why d'you say that?

Adam: Well, there's talk about you saving the planet. Aren't you concerned about the environment?

Josh: Of course, but the planet is people. I won't force people to change, I can't . . .

Adam: Oh, come on! You could snap your fingers and fix the ozone, couldn't you? Just like that. That's what all the papers say.

Josh: But that wouldn't stop deterioration happening again.

Adam: You could make it impervious to carbon emissions this time.

Josh: What? Do a better job on creation than the first time round, you mean? I think you're missing the point.

Adam: Which is?

Josh: The planet is people . . .

Adam: You've said that.

Josh: Yea, let me finish, people with the amazing gift of choice and freedom. We already have enough potential down here to make the difference.

Adam: You really think that? Sounds like a cop-out to me.

Josh: (rubbing his eyes with his fingers) People always want a quick fix. They want a heavenly provider who will sort out all their problems and relieve them of responsibility. But life revolves around respect, care, generosity, compassion, dignity, enthusiasm, humour, empathy – that's how it's designed. Life's like a plant – albeit a cactus or vine that can survive in the harshest conditions – but it still needs certain things to make it flourish. The cycle of normal life is all about work, rest, giving, taking, hospitality, trust . . .

Adam: Yea, but this is all very naïve. We're living in a harsh world, mate.

Josh: It's been a harsh world for a long time, Adam. Don't duck your responsibilities with that one.

Adam: So God won't help us? And you won't help us? We're gonna fry.

Josh: What are you talking about? Of course he'll help – but through people. That's his weapon of choice. Don't demand freedom if you don't want the responsibility. A lot is expected of those who are given much.

Adam: What's that supposed to mean?

Josh: If God made people for relationship then he had to give them freedom of choice, because no relationship is worth anything if you can't choose to step into it. Freedom of choice means the freedom to punch holes in the ozone, the freedom to ignore your neighbours, the freedom to talk more than do, the freedom to distort the truth, the freedom to only tell half a story, the freedom to choose greed over generosity, to build fortresses rather than hostels, castles instead of hospitals, the freedom to put living people on the moon and ignore dying ones on the earth.

Adam: That's a lot of bad news.

Josh: (rubbing his eyes again) I'm sorry, I'm tired. You're right – and I want to give good news;

there's plenty of good news. Maybe you could just tell the viewers you edited it out of the programme.

For the first time they both laugh.

Adam: Give us some good news, then.
Josh: No one's insignificant. How about that? In our fame-fuelled age even the invisible people are important. You may not ever get on the telly, you may not sing in a West End musical or have your own chat show. But those things often diminish your sense of significance anyway. Celebrate the small things. The best measure of greatness is your kindness to others. Fame is being known for a kind word and a smile. You may feel unworthy, stupid, clumsy, irretrievable, on the outside, but you're not. There's a kingdom coming – in fact it's here – it's all around, where the little people are the great ones. It doesn't come with Oscars and perfume and glamour; it's in the underworld, beneath the floorboards, in the cracks in the walls, down the back of the sofa, in the back alleys and side streets. It's everywhere, but you have to look and you have to learn the language. It's a kingdom where every little act of courage and kindness, every fleeting moment of heroism and every little endeavour to swim against the tide goes down in history and will be remembered forever. People look up there for heaven – to the skies, to other planets, to the stars and to aliens. It's in the other world down here, a parallel universe that runs alongside the façade of real life. The things that the media value – they mean

nothing. They'll be blown away like a handful of opium in the breeze. Yet every single moment of raising up another person, every micro second of compassion – that's solid gold.

Adam: (sighs) Well, I can't argue with that . . . Mainly cause I don't really get it! Did you have a thesaurus for lunch? Let's take some calls. Who's that?

There is the sound of a phone line clicking in.

Max: Hi, there's a few of us here actually. I'm Max.

Jake: I'm Jake.

Fiona: Hi, I'm Fiona – hi, Josh, love that thing you just said . . .

Max: Anyway, we saw what you'd been doing in Vietnam.

Adam: Cambodia.

Max: Cambodia, and well, we've got this mate, Ian and he's in a wheelchair. I know you were saying that, like, we can help each other and all that, and it's not about just asking God to do everything, but well – this is all we can do for him – call you.

Fiona: We never thought we'd get through – it's amazing!

Max: Yea, so, we're doing what we can – but can you do the rest, like? You made that guy see, that street guy who cleaned shoes.

Adam: Cut hair.

Max: Yea. Cut hair. So what d'you think?

Josh: Is Ian there?

Jake: Yea, he is, d'you want him?

Josh: Put him on the line.

Ian: Hi, Josh – look I didn't put them up to this, I really didn't. I have a great life, I have so many

	mates and I have a good job. I don't want you to feel sorry for me.
Josh:	I don't feel sorry for you, Ian. You sound like a great guy.
Ian:	Oh, I don't know about that . . .
Josh:	Don't put yourself down mate, you've got nothing to regret.
Ian:	Oh, I don't know about that either.
Josh:	Ian – your past is a clean slate, mate. It's all wiped clean. You can start again. You don't need to carry stuff round with you. You're a free man. You're crimes and misdemeanours – they're all gone.
Adam:	How can you say that when you don't know him?
Josh:	I know about his forgiveness.
Ian:	Cheers, mate!
Max:	Hang on – we phoned up for a miracle . . .
Fiona:	Yea, Max promised us Ian would be healed – not forgiven!
Josh:	Oh, don't blame Max. He didn't know Ian had been sinning!
Adam:	This is all getting very naïve.
Josh:	Naïve? Hmm. Yea, I guess so, there is a naivety about giving good things, there's a naivety about faith in God too. OK, Ian. Now, I'm about to walk into a lion's den because, of course, no one can see what's going on – but you and I know – and your mates will see, of course. Do me a favour, stand up for a moment, will you?

A pause on the line.

Ian:	What?
Josh:	Stand up, mate. I'm going to get so much stick about this forgiveness deal. So against my

better judgement I'm proving that God's on your side. Stand up and move about a bit.

Another pause on the line. An eternal one. Paint dries while we're waiting. Then . . .

Ian: Oh my . . .
Max: Shit! Oh, sorry. I mean – wow! He's standing.

There is the sound of laughing and clapping down the phone line.

Adam: Come on, Max, what's going on there?
Fiona: It's working, he's walking. Well actually, he's kicking a football – don't do that in here, Ian . . .

There is the sound of a window breaking.

Jake: Josh! You're the man! You done it, mate. Thanks – it's amazing – we knew you could do something.
Josh: My pleasure, mate. You'd better go and clean up that glass.
Max: No problem, we'll make Ian clean it up. In fact, he can clean the whole flat now that he can't pull a sickie any more. Cheers mate!

The phone clicks and the line shuts down.

Adam: (sharp intake of breath) People will say it was a scam.
Josh: Sure they will – but I didn't come here to prove anything. I don't care what they'll say. Ian's walking, and more importantly – he feels better about his past. Forgiveness is more powerful than a set of legs.

Adam: A set of legs gets you a long way.

Josh: Sure, in a society which favours the sleek and the swift.

Adam: So – what are you saying? We should all go round in wheelchairs? That doesn't make sense.

Josh: Of course not, but we're talking about the original nature of life.

Adam: Are we?

Josh: Yes. Like I said, where there's courage, kindness, grace, service, forgiveness, trust, heroism – that's normality. New legs wouldn't be that much good to Ian if he was crippled inside. There are many blind people who see far better than the sighted ones.

Adam: Well, nice platitude but I think we should see what our callers think . . . Oh, hang on (he listens to his earpiece). Really? Really! Wow! Well, apparently the phone lines are jammed. (he listens again) Apparently there's a fifty-fifty split between the people who love you and the people who'd like to see you on a spit roast for what you've just done.

Josh: There's a surprise.

Adam: Hang on. (listens to earpiece) Blimey! Apparently the PM's on the line – is this a wind-up? He's really on the line? Excellent! What a coup! Josh – it's the prime minister, right here on the Adam Clarke show – d'you want a word?

Josh: I doubt it'll do much good, but go ahead.

PM: Adam, thanks for taking my call.

Adam: No problem, sir, I wasn't up to much at the moment anyway. You want a word with Josh?

PM: I do, yes, is he there?

Adam: Sure. You're on.

PM: Josh?

Josh: Yes, Prime Minister?

PM: Word has travelled. I've heard an awful lot about you. Your reputation precedes you these days.

Josh: Sadly that's true. But I'm sure you know all about that.

PM: Josh, I'd love to get together with you sometime soon. I hear what you're saying about compassion and caring and making a difference. Your talents could be very helpful to government.

Josh: I'm not sure . . . I have a feeling my talents may have completely passed you by, Prime Minister.

PM: On the contrary – you may know there's another summit approaching. Something tells me you'd have the world's attention if you'd consider attending.

Josh: I don't want that kind of attention.

PM: But you do want to help save the planet.

Josh: Yes, one person at a time. You don't need summits for that.

PM: Josh, just think about it. I know what it's like on TV, the pressure, the attention, don't decide now. I'm not asking for a miracle, I hear what you're saying on that – I'm just asking for wisdom and inspiration.

Josh: Then I can do that now, Prime Minister. Don't abuse your power, respect the lowest person in your constituency. Don't lord it over people, don't worry about your reputation. Seek the good of the country, and start at the bottom. Be a servant, Mr Prime Minister.

PM: Nice advice, Josh, but let's talk.

Josh: I thought we just did.

PM: I'll be in touch.

Josh: (smiles) I'll be otherwise engaged.

Adam: Looks like he's playing hard to get, Prime Minister.

PM: I'll win him over.

Josh: Why? So you can win the next election?

PM: We're certainly looking good in the polls at the moment.

Josh: How good do you look in the mirror? When there's no one else around?

Adam: Ooh, careful Josh, you're talking to the First Gentleman here.

Josh: No I'm not. The First Gentleman is the guy on the street outside Broadcasting House who's drunk and alone because the corridors of power are carpeted with corruption.

PM: Josh – you have no idea what you're talking about.

Josh: Don't be so sure, Prime Minister. Let's just say, to quote a certain movie title, I know what you did last summer.

There is silence in the studio.

PM: (clears his throat) You'll be hearing from me, Josh. Thank you, Adam, goodnight.

Adam: Goodnight, Prime Minister.

There is a click and the line dies.

Adam: Well! What was that all about?

Josh: Who knows?

Adam: Well, I certainly don't, but I think I can see tomorrow's headlines making a dog's dinner of that particular horror flick. Sadly, we're nearly out of time and we have to wrap with that exclusive interview with the PM, but tell me one thing – there's something I don't get about all this. It seems you have all this power, this incredible supernatural talent to change things – yet you spend most of your time talking about us making a difference. Isn't that an abuse of your power – a denial of what you claim you're here to do?

Josh: If I heal people, it's to show them that they matter, that God cares. Because most people look through the wrong lens when they study God. If I do something good it's a sign, a clue to the nature of real life and the one who gives it. The answer to the world's troubles is not to have a divine conjuror. It requires a long-term solution and I'm not gonna be around forever.

Adam: Yea, but you've got a good . . . what . . . sixty years in you, fifty at least. I mean, if you get sick you can just (snaps fingers) fix yourself. You could live till you're like that old guy, Methuselah. How old was he – nine thousand and something?

Josh: Nine hundred and sixty-nine – but that's just the point. Methuselah lived so long because he was a sign to the people that God wants relationship. He was a walking message. Check out what Methuselah means: 'When he is dead – it'll be sent'. His very existence urged people that something was coming. Something they should take note of.

Adam: You've lost me.

Josh: Yea, I admit, I've digressed, and people don't really know the old stories. So many urban myths prevail . . . Anyway, the point is this. I don't have much longer, really I don't, so I can't be here fixing everything for everyone.

Adam: Where are you going?

Josh: (sighs) After this interview the heat will be on me. Death's waiting for me round the next bend.

Adam: Grief!! Don't go round it, then. Get a bus, take a train somewhere else.

Josh: I'd love to, believe me I'd love nine hundred and sixty-nine years of an easy life, but it all comes back to what I said. The world doesn't need another magician. A sacrifice is far more powerful.

Ninth Bit

Another town

'Sal? Sal, is that you? Yea, it's me, Tom. Josh gave me your number. He said I should call. I wanted to see you. Are you OK? Did you hear we went out on the road again? No, not abroad, just round here. I wanna tell you about it. Can I meet you? Come to the clearing. You know where some of us used to shoot? Behind the Old Mariner. It's a great place. The entrance is well concealed and you get lots of privacy. The Greyhound? OK, but the guys'll all be there. I wanted to spend some time with . . . you know . . . just you. I miss you, Sal. I'm sorry I didn't get in touch. It didn't mean I'd forgotten. Look, I don't know where we stand anyway, you know, with each other. Life's just weird at the moment, so much change. Can I see ya? Soon?'

Josh came out of hiding and we took a day trip to a different beach, a different town. Miz was there with her mate Jo. But not Sal; I still hadn't seen her. She wouldn't meet up after all. She'd been strange on the phone, guarded, distant. I noticed Jack and Miz were anything but distant. They seemed to have a good thing going.

It set me wondering if Si and Sal had something similar.

'I doubt it, dude,' said Nat when I muttered something to him. 'He's happily married.'

'You're kidding.'

'Nope. Josh fixed his old dear-in-law just last week. Total worst case, she was, dude comes along and bingo! Right as rain.'

I stopped and stared after him. We'd been walking up the beach and I stood still for a good few minutes before the grin smeared my face. If Si really was out of the running then nothing could stop us. Apart from me, of course.

'It's that guy off the telly!'

The yelling of kids brought me back to reality. A gang of teenagers was lolling by the sea wall. They got up and started running for us.

'Can we have your autograph?'

They crowded round the others while I hung back, thankful to be out of the crush.

Josh pulled a pen and scribbled on their shirts, arms and comic books. A crowd draws a crowd and before you could say *I'm a Celebrity – Get Me Out of Here*, shopkeepers and sunbathers were spilling across the sand to see what was going on.

'It's him! The miracle man.'

This one kid had such a big voice. I so wanted to fill his mouth with damp sand.

Before you knew it the beach was crowded and Josh had a good old-fashioned gig going on, joking with the kids and launching into his famous runaway boy story.

'Hey!'

This new voice came from nowhere. The kids looked around, we all looked around.

'I said, hey!'

It was like the voice of God booming from the sky. I glanced up. A guy on a hang glider was coming at us right out of the sun.

'Watch out!' he warned and people scattered.

He steered a clumsy way down and landed in an undignified pile of silk and safety harness. When he stood up and fought his way out of the carnage the first thing I noticed was he was wearing one heck of a sharp suit.

'I'm Zac Temple,' he said, walking over to Josh with his hand out.

A big smile filled his features, but he was the only one grinning.

'What's he doing here?' someone muttered.

He ignored it. The crowd began to close in again.

'Don't waste your time with him, Josh. He's a born loser.'

'I think you'll find you lot are the losers,' the man snapped. 'I'm the one in the Armani suit.'

He was, too. And in spite of the rumblings in the crowd, people were eyeing him with nervous caution, no one wanting to get too close.

Josh looked him up and down.

'You got a good living round here?' Josh asked.

And everyone laughed.

'No,' someone said, 'we *had* a good living and he rips us off.'

'Yea! Pimping, loan sharking, debt collecting, protection rackets. He's nothing if not diverse.'

Zac ignored them. He and Josh studied one another.

'Where d'you live?' Josh asked.

The crowd sneered.

'Wherever he wants.'

'I've heard a lot about you,' Zac Temple said.

'And?'

'If you can convince me you're for real – then I'm interested.'

'I'm not selling anything, Mr Temple.'

'I'm not buying. I saw you on the Adam Clarke show.' He pursed his lips for a second then said, 'I liked what you said about real life.'

'You're full of something but it ain't real life,' someone jeered.

The crowd laughed but Josh held up his hand.

'We need to talk without an audience,' he said. 'Where d'you live?'

'You're kidding!' It was the kid with the megaphone voice. 'Don't waste your time with that scumbag.'

Josh scratched his head and looked around at the crowd.

'I came for scumbags,' he said, 'not for the good guys.'

'I'm a scumbag,' said the kid with the voice, and I was inclined to agree. Me and the whole beach.

Josh wouldn't be deterred. He left the muttering crowd and wandered off into the morning with the man in the Armani suit. The people muttered and cussed and scattered while the kids went back to lolling on the beach.

We all looked at one another.

'I'm hungry,' said Si.

So, like sheep, we went looking for somewhere cheap and plentiful.

The Business was just that – a pub with good beer and solid nourishment. We got in a good hour's drinking before Josh found us.

'What happened to Zac?' Andy asked.

Josh grinned and pulled a wad of notes from his pocket.

'He's buying you lunch.'

'What?'

'He's had a change of heart. I'm going to study the porcelain. Get me pie and chips, will you?'

So we did. And we waited for him. And we waited. Then we got another round in. And another. The pie and chips went cold so we ate them and drank his pint.

'Maybe he's been mugged,' Nat said eventually.

Si grabbed Andy and, for some reason, Andy grabbed me.

'Let's sort this out,' he said.

The toilets were beyond a back room so we went on through. And stopped dead in our tracks.

Josh was in there – alone with a beautiful woman. Standing very close to her.

We stared.

'Josh, sorry, we thought . . .'

We turned and left and sat down. No one said a thing.

'What happened?'

Nat and the others looked at us.

Miz said, 'You lot look like you've seen a ghost.'

Then Josh walked in. Alone.

'Sorry,' he said. 'I got distracted.'

We said nothing. Her perfume was hanging around his clothes. He pulled more of Zac's money from his pockets.

'Anyone for another round?'

'I think we need it,' said Si.

The start of the end

I'll admit it shook me. He'd been so long in there. She was beautiful and we heard later that she was the town bicycle. Why should it bother me? He was a regular guy. What was the problem? One day I'd ask him about it. He'd tell me, I'm sure he would.

'Sal, it's me. Who's that? Oh, I thought it was Sal. Can I speak to her? Why not? How bad? But she was fine! Oh, it's Tom, no we've not met, but well, she's become a bit of a good friend. Can I not just have a quick word? Just so . . . Oh! Really? What d'you mean? Oh my . . . I'm sorry. I had no idea, I . . . Yea. Bye.'

Sal was in hospital. It was the start of the end for her.

As the summer picked up the weather finally kicked in, the pavements grew hot and the days burned bright.

The way into the clearing behind the Old Mariner was well concealed. The break in the fence sat behind a rhododendron bush and the opening was covered by a loose piece of hinged plasterboard that fell back over the hole every time we passed through.

Occasionally one or two kids would find the way in and stick their heads through but they soon scarpered when they saw the likes of us hanging around.

I began going there on my own in the evenings. I'd take a can of Guinness and sit in the grass with my back against one of the many palm trees, planted by the hotel once upon a time. There was a complete ring of them on the edge of the clearing, fifteen including the two that had been uprooted by the wind. I guess the owners of the hotel had designed the clearing so people could lie there and think of paradise. I'd pretend I was back in Cambodia, living another kind of life. A life where Sal was well and it was always hot and I was successful doing something or other; a life where I was never lonely or stuck on the edge. In my mind I heard again the sounds of crickets, tree hoppers and cicadas, I watched lizards slither in the grass and wild monkeys playing in the trees. The seagulls were parakeets and I'd swap my can of G for a green coconut and a straw.

Stupid really. Cause I doubt if I'd really like it there. And Sal wasn't getting better. But it was a dream I could visit every day. Maybe this clearing was enough of paradise for me. I   didn't have to board a plane and pack the bags. Problem was, I knew winter was coming. The blue skies would go and the sunsets would die and instead of the cool breeze on my face there'd be a biting wind and sheets of freezing rain. And it wasn't only the sunsets that would die.

Jill

I was sitting in the clearing one evening when Josh dropped by. I heard a rustle in the trees and the cracking of twigs and I turned to see him leaning on a beach tree grinning at me.

'It's been a long and winding road, Tom,' he said, 'a long and winding road.'

I nodded.

'And it's about to get a lot more difficult.'

'It already has,' I said.

He sat beside me and started tossing spent shotgun cartridges at an empty beer can.

'Tom, if you could go anywhere, do anything, money no object, what would you do?'

So I told him about my paradise in Cambodia. The cicadas and the monkeys and the green coconuts.

'Tom,' he said, 'you may still get there, mate.'

'You've changed a lot, Josh. You're not the kid who helped me fill in that business start-up form.'

He laughed. 'And you're not the guy who wanted to con the government out of some beer money.'

I blushed. 'It wasn't just a scam. Part of me was serious about the woodcarving idea.'

He held up a hand. 'I know, mate, don't worry, that's all dead and gone now. Which brings me to my reason for dropping by. I may be dead and gone soon, too.'

'What?'

'You know what it's been like lately, so much pressure from people. Pressure to do the right thing . . . say the right thing . . . be the right thing. They want me to go up to London for this summit. I can't do it, Tom. I don't know how much you understand what's been going on. But I can't just play the popularity game.'

'Can I ask you something?'

'Go ahead. I have a feeling this may be our last chance for a serious head-to-head.'

'What were you doing with that girl? The one in The Business the other week?'

He smiled and nodded. 'Yea, didn't look good, did it? The thing is, Tom, if you're gonna show people they matter, you have to take risks. She'd been so messed about and used by people, especially guys, I wanted to show her that she was worth more than her body. She's an amazing lady, highly intelligent. I had to work hard to keep up with her.' He laughed to himself. 'If it matters to you, Tom, nothing happened – and thank goodness it didn't, it would have been disastrous for both of us.' He wiped a trickle of sweat from his forehead. The evening was close, it was gonna be a warm night. 'That isn't the first time I've had to battle the temptation. Did you know I disappeared for a while?'

'At the start of the summer?'

'Yea. Well, that was the beginning. Money, sex, power. I went off to face all that, and it nearly killed me. I needed to sort it out in my head. Know that I was gonna do all this for the right reasons. It's so easy to chase fame, to be flattered by others and believe the applause. You've got crap on your shoes, mate, let me get that off.'

'What?'

He knelt down and yanked off my trainer, and before I could stop him he'd picked up a handful of leaves and was scraping off the foul mess.

'You don't need to do that . . .'

He ignored me.

'It didn't make it easier when I was standing with Jill in that pub, though,' he said as he worked. 'And it didn't make it any easier whenever I saw Sal and Miz and Jo . . .' and he gave me a shy smile. 'The summer's a natural aphrodisiac, eh, Tom? But having faced it out on my own at the start – it made it . . .' he paused and considered, then said, 'possible.' He sighed and handed me back the clean shoe. Then suddenly he groaned and his whole body seemed to cave in as he did it. He dropped to the ground and pulled his knees to his chest.

'I sometimes wish I'd never started this,' he said, rocking back and forth on his backside. 'So many lonely nights, so many misunderstandings . . .'

Something in me snapped.

'You have to keep going,' I barked, and he looked at me, startled. 'You have to. You can't stop now. Where would we all go? Think about it.'

He looked up at me, pain in his eyes.

'Come on, Josh.' I pulled on his shoulder. 'You can do it.'

He kept staring for a moment, his eyes wide and fixed on something else, something beyond me. Then suddenly he blinked twice and laughed. 'Yea, sure. Thanks, Tom. You're right, course I can.'

'You have to.'

'Yea. I have to.' He stood up and dusted the sand from his jeans. 'I have to,' he repeated.

He started to leave.

'Josh,' I called, pulling on the trainer, 'there's a reason I said that.'

A blanched, brittle shell

They'd brought Sal home – there was nothing more to do, and her dad wanted her to die where she'd grown up.

I called them the day they moved her into her bedroom, the room she'd slept in since she was three.

'Mr Green, it's Tom. Look, this is a long shot and I don't want to prolong your agony . . .'

He came to my flat and I'd arranged for Josh to be there to meet him. Trouble was, Josh was late. And it was just me and Sal's dad, standing there in the dark. Then the call came. The one neither of us wanted, the worst news in the world. There was still no sign of Josh and it had to be me alone trying to think of something to say to comfort this businessman I'd never met before. He was the most dignified man I'd ever met, silver grey hair, twinkling eyes, warm smile. Like Father Christmas in a pinstriped suit. I could see where Sal got her good nature from.

Then Josh came.

'You're late,' I snarled at him.

'I know, I'm sorry,' he said.

'Too late,' I said.

Sal was dead.

Her dad made for the door.

'Thanks for trying, Tom,' he muttered, his voice weak and dry, 'but I need to get back now. Sal's mum'll be in a dreadful state.'

He was stumbling as he went; he could barely see for the grief in his eyes.

'Wait.'

It was Josh.

'It isn't over,' he said. 'I'm coming with you.' A pause. 'If that's OK?'

So we snuck in the back of Jerry Green's Audi and sat in silence as he sobbed quietly in the front. I couldn't think straight; a huge part of me was falling to pieces inside, but the other part, the public bit, had moved into 'I'm not going to show any weakness' autopilot.

'It'll do no good,' I whispered. 'What will we say to them all? Whatever you do, don't offer them one of your stories.'

Josh raised a hand. 'Shut up,' he said, so I did.

Sal looked like a shell – a blanched, brittle shell. She looked smaller and unreal. Josh stood two steps from the bed, wedged between her parents. I hung back by the door. Outside there were hushed confused voices. Two strangers walk into your house and demand to see the still warm body of your dead daughter. Perfectly natural thing to do.

Josh moved closer to the body. Everything seemed wrong. Why did I think getting him involved would be a good idea? These people just needed to grieve now. I willed him to move away. He didn't. Instead he leant over Sal, my Sal, the girl who'd started to bring me back from the dead, the girl I desperately needed alive. In those few moments I realised what had started to happen to me; suddenly it was as if she represented everything – the future, the past, the desire to keep fighting the old me, the chance that life might work out OK. I gritted my teeth and pictured a solid brick wall in my mind; I needed to stop thinking, stay detached. I couldn't let this get to me, couldn't let these people see what was really going on.

I'd stood beside another bed twenty years ago, and so many of my hopes had died with the body back then. There was too much resting on this.

'Sal, wake up!'

'What are you doing?' Her mother was clawing at Josh's jacket. 'Leave her alone!'

She started screaming and slapping his shoulder to push him back. Behind us, someone opened the door to see what was going on.

'Close the door,' said Josh quietly. 'Sal, wake up. Come on.'

He placed his hands on her cold cheeks. He pinched her lower lip and moved her chin.

'Breathe! Come on. Sal! I'm talking to you.'

Mr Green reached out to stop Josh. Enough was enough. I buried my face and turned away. No one noticed as I slipped out of the door.

So this was it. The dream was over. Sal, Josh, the future. All gone in a few desperate minutes. Well, it had been good while it lasted. People asked me questions as I pushed through the house but I answered no one. I walked outside and felt the first spots of rain.

Miz was standing in the garden, her face flushed and her eyes red. Without even thinking, I put my arm round her. She didn't fight it off.

'I had a brother,' I said, 'a twin. He died when I was twelve. It wrecked my life. Why did he have to die? Why do people do that? Why's it all happening again now? Why? I don't wanna hear his platitudes about the king-dom coming amongst the trouble. I've had a shed-load of trouble. I don't want any more. I want it to be over. I want it over . . . Enough!'

Miz had no idea what I was rambling on about but she squeezed my arm anyway. She cried and I stared and the rain made both our faces wet.

Why?

'Come on.'

There was a hand on my shoulder. It was Josh.

'Come on.'

'I'm not going anywhere with you.'

'You are, mate. There's someone to see you.'

'Where?'

'Inside. Now!'

He yanked me back into the house and I pulled Miz with me. He pushed his way back to the bedroom. The nearer we got, the louder the wailing got. I wasn't going back in there. No way.

'Get in!'

He shoved me hard, so hard that my body thumped through the door and I collided with the bed.

Sal was gone. They must have carted her away. Sal's sister was standing on the far side of the room, staring out of the window looking very lost. I didn't know what to do. Then I realised they weren't wailing. They were screaming and laughing and shouting. Someone called my name.

'Tom!'

Sal's sister turned and smiled at me. Why was she smiling? Then she started saying something to me from across the room as I stared at the empty bed and tried to work out what all the noise was about. I squinted at her. And then the penny dropped.

It wasn't Sal's sister. It was Sal. There by the window. There was no dead girl. It was really Sal. Upright and breathing. Next thing, she was laughing and hugging Miz and talking about feeling hungry.

It took me a while to recover. I was so torn up inside, worn out from trying to keep the grief buried, that it was hard to connect with the celebration that swirled like fog around me. Other people were laughing and crying and clapping and jumping about. I just stood there watching from inside this bubble. Sal hugged me and I held her for a long time and then someone else whisked her away and shoved a drink in my hand. The party went on for a long time.

Eventually, Josh took me back to my flat and we sat in silence for a while and then he dropped the bomb.

'I know about Mike, Tom. I know you struggled to be him, to replace him for your dad. No wonder you hid in the drink – that's too much for any guy.'

I looked hard at him.

'Do you want to talk about him?'

I shook my head.

He nodded and turned away, and suddenly I blurted it out: 'Why did he have to die?'

He considered this, flicked at a broken fingernail and nodded for a while. Why was he nodding? There was nothing to nod about.

'Would it really help you to know?' he asked.

'He messed up my life, Josh. Big time. Massive. Complete cock-up in my head. I was doing all right till that happened. Then he went and died and it all fell apart. Afterwards I tried to do well at school, then at uni, but I couldn't be him. He was the intelligent one, the sporty one, the funny one. It was all him, not me. I tried and I tried and I bloody tried. And in the end I just gave up.'

I swore. A genuine torrent of stagnant abuse, aimed at no one but me and my years of failure. He didn't bat an eyelid, waited for me to burn out, to finish spewing the poison, then he spoke quietly.

'But now you've got another chance, Tom. You couldn't bring Mike back – but you brought Sal back.'

'I didn't, you did.'

'But it was your faith in me.'

I sneered. 'Faith? I doubt it. I've got more questions than *The Times* crossword.'

He smiled. 'Faith isn't what you think, it's what you do. And today you took me to see a dead girl.'

'It's the guilt,' I said, 'that's the worst part.'

'The guilt?'

'Yea, some days I felt glad he'd gone – while he was alive, he just put me in the shade all the time. Other days I felt bad cause I could have saved him.'

'What d'you mean?'

'He had a seizure, went into a fit and smacked his head on the ground. We were messing about in this park. No one else around. I left him unconscious by the swings. I went to get help but I didn't run fast enough, by the time I got back it was too late. I just can't remember whether I slowed up deliberately.'

'You did what you could, Tom.' He paused then said, 'This world's a bad place, Tom.'

'Yea, yea, you said already . . .'

'Let me finish. There are not enough good things to say to make it better. Not enough explanations to soothe the pain. All we can do is live and demonstrate that there's more. More than the hard roads in life.'

I shrugged. I'd think about whatever he'd just said on a better day.

'Terrible things happen. Right now something bad is happening to loads of people. Soon, something bad'll happen to me . . .'

'Stop saying that! Why d'you keep saying that?'

'I'm trying to prepare you.'

'I don't want to be prepared.'

'I'm going to this summit, Tom, and I know that something will happen.'

'Then don't go. Don't stand there preparing me, just don't go.'

'Tom, I had all this with Si. You know I have to go. Don't argue with me on this.'

'But you said you weren't interested in it.'

'I changed my mind.' He sighed and ran a hand through his hair. 'Please don't make it difficult. It's hard enough anyway without you trying to stop me.'

So I didn't. I just said nothing at all. After a while, he made for the door.

He froze with his hand on the catch.

'I go in a few days,' he said. 'Will you come to the clearing next week – on Thursday night? All the guys'll be there . . .' Pause. 'Sal will be there too.'

I nodded, it was the faintest of nods, but I complied.

He opened the door and went.

Tenth Bit

Chat shows and foetal scans

The news about Sal spread quickly. It was such an awesome thing people couldn't ignore it. It seemed to notch everything up to another level. We all started getting letters from folk who had rellies who were sick or dying. Andy kept getting emails after a reporter leaked his address – on one day alone, two thousand came in from all over. Jack was getting texts from Africa. It was all going ballistic.

I felt weird about the whole thing, if I'm honest. I wanted Sal to be alive so much, but when what had happened really sunk in, it seemed insane. I knew people had near-death experiences and all that – but having the power to talk 'em back from the far side? That was well off-limits. I began to see why Josh didn't like miracles – they screwed things up. They turned him into Derren Brown, David Blaine and Paul Daniels all rolled into one. Everybody wanted a piece of him. It was like the Diana madness times a thousand. Wherever he went people snipped at his clothes, and yanked out bits of his hair. One woman came at him with a carving knife and hacked off so much of his hair he had to have an emergency restyle. People seemed to think bits of his body could solve their problems. In the following week there were twenty-six documentaries screened on TV about him. People sent him clothes of their dead family members so he could resurrect 'em fully dressed. We opened a Jiffy bag one day to find it stuffed full of ashes. It was the remains of someone's long-departed grandparents, but the ashes were so mixed up that the result might well have been a terrifying two-headed, eight-limbed freak. People posted their dead pets, kids sent decomposing goldfish. Josh was asked to bless their football boots and cricket bats, swimming caps and chess sets; while their parents sent photos of missing family members hoping for a map reference by return of post. We got foetal scans, prescriptions, confidential medical reports and incomprehensible X-rays; not to mention calendars and diaries of would-be parents, describing in fascinating detail the dates and times and techniques of their forthcoming sexual activities.

We were offered chat shows, game shows, talent shows, film deals, a mini-series, even recording contracts. Sal had never recorded a song in her life but she was confidently offered a sackful of inappropriate cover versions relating to her brush with the afterlife, including 'Say a Little Prayer', 'I Get Knocked Down but I Get Up Again', 'Bat Out of Hell', 'Heaven Must Be Missing an Angel', 'Wake Me Up Before You Go-Go', 'Don't Leave Me This Way', 'You Raise Me Up' and my personal favourite, 'Die Another Day'.

Men in sharp suits started appearing. And we'd get calls from people calling themselves Mr Jones and Miss Smith who 'just wanted a quick word with him'. Occasionally we'd be tailed by gleaming black people carriers with tinted windows. Stretch limos would pull up and chauffeurs would stick their heads out of the window and beckon us with gloved fingers. It was a strange and macabre time. It really was.

I felt strange towards Josh after the last conversation we'd had. He was fine with me – he was always fine, it was really irritating – he never felt the need to harbour grudges. But I'm the kind who keeps replaying stuff in my head and I kept re-running the conversation about Mike over and over again. I felt exposed. Embarrassed that he knew so much. I wanted to retract the information, erase the film that contained the footage of me talking about my brother.

And this guy Keats kept hanging around. I didn't know him but Jack and Jimmy did. Nasty piece of work, they said. In league with all kinds of lowlife. Always wore a long black leather coat and shades, whatever the weather. He ran a string of garages all over the county but he looked as if he hadn't changed a spark plug in a very long time. He always had two minders with him, real pretty boys. Wallace and Gromit, we called 'em. Wallace was tall, pale, northern and had a deceptive vacant grin. Gromit was squat, short, tattooed and had a neck like a bulldog. Straight out of a comic book, all three of them. Keats was looking to get in with Josh, sniffing about for favours. I guess he recognised power when he saw it.

'I'm a good churchman,' he'd say whenever he passed near us. 'Devout and pious. Never miss a Sunday.'

Yea, right. Whatever.

Temple raiding

The night after everything with Sal, I slept badly. In fact, the next four nights were not good. I escaped all the hype, stocked up on booze and hid in my flat. I visited my old lover, Sky Scandinavian Three, but she somehow wasn't as stunning as I remembered. Sal called a couple of times and I tried to sound upbeat, but I couldn't tell her what was really going on in the dark recesses of my head. I said I'd see her soon, and she said, 'Not if I see you first.' But we didn't make any plans.

When Saturday came, I was sitting alone on the seafront, nursing a headache and watching the sun come up.

'What the . . .'

I jerked round as I felt a hand on my shoulder. Jude was there.

'Big day today, Tom,' he said and he offered me a cigarette.

'You know I don't smoke,' I said.

'Really? Oh no, it's just the booze for you, isn't it?'

'Not even that, I'm giving up.'

'Brave man,' he said.

'No, I'm a coward.'

'Well, steel yourself, because today we're going global.'

'What?'

Jude held up his video camera and patted the lens cover.

'Josh's riding into Truro on my BMW. The place'll be jammed. They'll be eating out of his hand and the media will love it.'

I laughed. 'You're kidding me. Truro – hardly the centre of the known world.'

'Nope. But he is. Trust me, Tom, right now you can sell footage of him all over the planet.' He pulled a wad of notes from his pocket. 'Need cash?' he said, but I shook my head. I was beginning to regret my dependency on him. I had a hunch it might blow up in my face one day.

'What's in Truro, then?' I said.

'A cathedral, and you know how he loves those – my guess is he'll do some more temple raiding.'

'You love this don't you, you're lapping it up . . . What's that under your arm?'

Jude glanced down at the FedEx parcel.

'Just some stuff,' he said.

I knew it wasn't.

'Where's that guru of yours?'

We looked round. It was Keats, but unusually he was alone. Not even a pit bull in tow. Keats always had a pit bull.

'Why d'you wanna know?' asked Jude.

'I want a word on the discreet with him.'

'We don't know where he is,' I butted in. 'He often takes time out on his own.'

'He's on the beach,' said Jude.

How did he know these things?

He nodded over my shoulder and sure enough, there on the sand was Josh, picking up stones and skimming them on the water. I'd like to tell you now, for the record, that he was throwing them like no one on earth, bouncing them all the way from here to the next continent. But I can't. He wasn't. He was chucking them like any other bloke, worse than some, in fact.

Keats nodded in his direction and shoved a cheroot in his mouth.

'He's so comic book, that guy,' I said as he sauntered off.

'Not when he's kicking the living daylights out of another human being,' said Jude. 'I've seen it.'

For the audience

Maybe it was for that reason that we tagged along, just to keep an eye out. Not obviously of course, just nonchalantly, which means as nonchalant as normal people are when they're trying to look nonchalant. However we looked, Jude and I strolled in the same direction.

We missed the first part of the conversation but we rolled up for the most interesting bit.

'I thought I told you this was on the discreet,' Keats said when he saw us.

'They're my closest friends,' said Josh. 'They won't disclose our conversation.'

'Well if they do, they'll be sucking food through a straw for a long time.'

Josh shrugged. 'This is what I'm talking about, Mr Keats. You can say all the right things, be seen in all the right places. But most of what we say in public is just done for the audience in any given situation.'

'Don't belittle me like that,' Keats said, with a flush in his cheeks. 'I give more money away than you've ever seen. I can recite the Commandments and if I break them I apologise and I make amends. Everyone breaks the rules. Everyone lies, everyone's selfish. At least I'm upfront about it.'

'Not everyone threatens other people with violence.'

'True. You got me on that one. But this is what I'm saying. At my time in life I'm willing to consider change.'

'You mean you're getting older and you're scared of death?'

'Don't push me, kid. This is hard enough for me. Give me room to manoeuvre.' Keats cleared his throat and spat in the sand. The gob of spit was very discoloured indeed. 'If I stop . . . what I do . . . I'll be comfortable now. More than that, I could be very benevolent. I think I could make a difference to the planet.'

'Would you indulge me for a minute? I have a story for you.'

'Not that one again about the kid who runs away . . .'

'No, but it's another one about brothers. A man has two grown-up sons. He asks for their help to fix his car. The older boy agrees and intends to do it. But then he gets distracted, starts on other things, and never gets round to it. The old man asks the other boy. And he's just a reckless punk. "No way," the kid says. "Got better things to do." However, the young punk thinks again, gets up, goes out and fixes the car. Result. The question is which one did what his father wanted?'

Keats sighed. 'We both know the answer to that . . . the younger one.'

'Exactly, even though the older boy had all the right words. So which are you, Mr Keats? The older or the younger? You know, I don't think you really ever wanted to hurt anyone. I guess that was just a means to an end. So this is my advice – forget about money. Switch your thinking. Don't retire comfortably. Get rid of the motivations in your life which lead you to a life of crime. Lose the cash.'

Keats looked as if he'd just been asked to donate his left arm.

'What . . . what are you on about?'

'Think about it. Do the right thing. Care for the poor and the broken, sit down with them in the gutters and under the bridges. Get to know the weak for a while. Can you do that?'

Keats shook his head. 'I own a football team!' he said. 'I got responsibilities. People depend on me.' He shook his head again. 'I don't understand, I came to you in all good faith willing to rethink my life. But instead you give me riddles and stories and you treat me like an idiot.'

'Do I?'

Keats didn't reply. He just turned back and followed his footsteps across the sand.

Josh looked at us and spoke sadly. 'Many people talk the talk and make it sound impressive. Most of the people who walk the walk don't say much about it. It's hard for people like Keats, he's got so much between him and life. And the irony is, he calls the baggage life. People were made to be loved and things to be used. Not the other way round. Come on, let's go to Casualty.'

A hell of an impact

We walked. And Josh pulled his hood up. It was like that now. He couldn't be seen in public without it causing some kind of stir. We stood at the back of the casualty ward and Jude and I stood in front of Josh to shield him. It was a busy morning already and the place was full of welts, black eyes, DIY wounds and surfing injuries. Everyone was staring at the information boards.

The girl at the desk spotted us and called us over. Jude went to see her, his FedEx parcel still wedged under his arm.

'She wants to know why we haven't checked in,' he said when he came back.

'Cause we don't want a room,' Josh said, pushing his hood down so he could case the joint.

Jude's face cracked a massive grin. 'When you gonna do it, then?' he asked.

'Do what?'

'You know, the big one.'

'He's right,' I said. 'You could make a hell of an impact here.'

Josh stared at us, open-mouthed. 'I think we've already made a pretty big impact, don't you? I can't even go the bathroom without someone following me so they can take away a relic of whatever I deposit there.'

Jude stepped away, exposing Josh. 'You mean – you didn't come here to cure everybody? Come on! Just snap your fingers – that's all it takes. You know you want to.'

Josh was getting frustrated now. 'Why do you always want more miracles? Haven't you seen enough?' He grabbed Jude and yanked him back into place. 'You guys don't get it, do you? How many times . . . It's not miracles that matter – it's *people*. I'm not here to prove anything.'

'What are you here for, then?'

As Jude stepped away again, a middle-aged hippie looked over from his seat in the corridor. No one else batted an eyelid but the guy kept staring. He was wearing a T-shirt that said 'I hate you'.

'Oh-oh, you've been spotted,' I said.

'Then that's who I'm here for.'

Josh pulled up his hood and went over and sat beside the guy.

I didn't know what to make of it all. He seemed irritable and that was unlike Josh.

'Don't worry,' said Jude, 'it's just a blip. I have a cunning plan.' And he tapped his finger to his temple and left me.

I hung around for a while and watched. I couldn't help thinking it had to be me that had made things hard for Josh. He chatted to the middle-aged guy for quite a while, then he bent over and disappeared from view. When he straightened he was holding a set of callipers. The hippie stood up, gripped Josh's shoulder and ambled off, dumping a pair of sticks in a nearby waste bin as he went. Josh watched him leave, fixed his shades and hastily sidled back over towards me looking for all the world like Bono's younger brother.

'Come on,' he said, pulling up his hood, 'let's get out of here.'

We ran, literally, all the way down the high street –
dodging cars and tripping over trolleys, it was like a
scene from *Trainspotting*. When we reached the seafront,
we stopped and stood gasping and checking our backs.
Nothing. No one was after him. He pointed to a nearby
café and we went inside and ordered fresh coffee and a
pile of toast.

Pancakes

He didn't mention my brother and I felt the better for it.
We laughed about lots of stupid things and I asked him
where he got all his stories from.

'I have thousands up here,' he said. 'I've been storing
them up for years. I have more than I'll ever tell, and
more than people can stand too. That's the thing, I'd
love to tell some of them but it would be too much for
people. It would be like dropping your iPod in front of a
steamroller – it would be a daft thing to do. People
would misunderstand and react badly. So I have to filter
what I reveal. But stories are such a great way to pass on
powerful secrets. If you just serve up truth on a plate
those that are on your side will merely nod and smile
and forget it, those that are against you will shut it out
and give it no more air time. Stories hang around, they
get passed on, they stay with people, they entertain and
annoy. Truth lurks in the gaps between the words and
phrases and if you chew on the tale long enough the
goodness oozes out and infects your being and then
you're in danger of changing forever. Sermon over. I'm
still hungry . . . those pancakes on the next table look
good. Let's order some.'

'Jude said you're going to Truro on the back of his
bike?'

He laughed. 'That's what Jude thinks. He's trying so hard to stage-manage me – I think he has a plan to see me at the London Palladium, there or Wembley.'

'So are you going to Truro?'

He waved to the waitress and I waited while she came over and they chatted for a while. He was only ordering pancakes but he took five minutes to find out her name was Natalie, she was studying to be a vet, had four younger brothers to mother and was in love with Paul Merton.

'What did you ask me?' he said as she walked away.

'Was that a chat-up or what?' I asked.

He laughed. 'You decide,' he said. 'Now, Truro. Yea, you see there's an old saying about a leader riding humbly into a city. A different kind of leader, I suppose. Kind of a sign of hope and peace.'

'So why not ride into London?'

'Because I'd get stuck in traffic. It'd take all day and no one would see for the fumes.'

'But you are going to London?'

Natalie returned with the pancakes and a winning smile. He swapped jokes with her and he introduced me. It was odd, Josh and I were the mates but I felt like I was intruding on something.

She left and he doused a plate of bacon and pancakes in Canadian syrup.

'Man, you are hungry!' I said.

'I got a big day ahead.'

'What is this London thing?'

'The Gore Summit – it's an international environmental thing. Lots of leaders looking good for the cameras and spending a lot of time talk, talk, talking.'

'But you're not interested in that. I thought you said you weren't bothered about the environment.'

'Easy! I never said that. I just think the way to change the planet is one head at a time. Those guys are the ones who can adjust policy – I can only meet people.'

'They won't wanna hear that.'

'You reckon.'

'They'll want you to make some great speech about how we should all recycle our toilet paper and skateboard everywhere.'

He shrugged. 'You gotta do what you can.'

I looked at him for a while. I just didn't get it. He looked like any other guy right there, tucking into breakfast with a fervour; his hoodie skewed at the neck, Canadian syrup on his unshaved chin and bags under his eyes. He looked older now, way older than when we'd first met; I guess we both did. He seemed wiser, though. I didn't.

'A euro for your thoughts,' he said, and he pushed the pancakes towards me. 'And eat! You got a mountain to climb today.'

'How can you sit there like this?'

'Like what?'

'Like you're not the guy who just fixed some hippie's legs. He probably hadn't walked for a decade . . .'

'Two, actually.'

'All right, two. And you come along and give him a smile and a handshake and he's up and off. He'll be running the marathon next year. And in the meantime you go on your merry way – making magic burgers, giving legs to people who beg for alms, and bringing people back to . . . you know . . .' I tailed off. He kept eating. He waved his knife at me.

'How is Sal, by the way? Is it going good for you two?'

I shrugged. 'I dunno. I . . . I . . . I don't know how to do this kind of thing. I'm not used to this. Sometimes I feel like she could ditch me any day, you know?'

He leaned across and jabbed me in the forehead with his fork. It hurt.

'Yea, right, you lost cause. Don't worry, you ain't Mr Bean. She won't give you up.'

'You can't say that, someone else might come along. She might change her mind.'

He stopped chewing, narrowed his eyes and wiped a hand across his chin.

'Tom, she can see in you what I can see in you.'

'Oh, don't tell me that. Don't say that. If that's true I haven't got a hope.'

'You aren't going to be around here forever, mate. Whatever you might think, you're on the up. You're going somewhere. She can see that, and she's prepared to go with you.'

'Just so long as I don't mess it up.'

He shrugged. 'Mess it up if you like. Love ain't about getting it right. I know her, trust me. She'll stick with you.' He forked a pancake and flung it on my plate. 'Eat!'

'It's all so straightforward with you,' I snapped. 'Like you know everything.'

'I didn't know the pancakes here were this good. I didn't know I was gonna meet that guy in the hospital. I didn't know I was gonna get the Spanish Inquisition over breakfast.' He winked at me and I gave up. We poured coffee, swallowed the rest of the food and finished up.

'All right, then, if I'm on the up, where am I going?' I asked as he signalled Natalie for the bill.

He grinned. 'A hell of a long way from here.'

And that scared me stupid.

Wham bam

While Josh went off to make a private call I hung around on the front waiting for the others. Word had gone out and everyone was gonna show at 11 a.m. to catch the train to Truro. It all seemed yet another bizarre twist in this never-ending story. I had no idea that the never-ending bit was about to change big time.

Nat and Matt turned up first. Matt was wearing his iPod and singing along to everything from Hot Chocolate to Coldplay.

'Hey!' He yelled over the music which only he could hear, 'I found this great book in Oxfam – *1,000 Things You Should Know About Bird Flu* – fascinating.'

The poor guy was addicted to minor irritating facts about life. The three of us stood around waiting, Nat filling the air with unnecessary clichés.

Then Matt's phone went off. He flipped it open and studied the screen. It was a dead ringer for one of those old *Star Trek* communicators.

'Oh great,' Matt muttered.

'What is it?'

'It's Anja, she's ovulating again.'

'What?'

'My wife.'

We had no idea. Well, we often didn't bother with such minor details, personal life and all that.

'She's desperate for a kid,' he said and he started to text her back. 'It's a nightmare. Sex used to be great. Now it's like taking your driving test.'

Nat and I frowned at each other. We'd just learned more about Matt in the last four sentences than the past four months.

'It's so unfair – if you're fifteen all you need is a Bacardi Breezer and a quickie behind the bike sheds and wham bam! You're pregnant. Once you're married, you've gotta get the date right, the time, the temperature, the angle and the colour of the bedroom walls. Getting it on with Anja's like filling in a tax return.'

'Worst case scenario, dude, you should have a word with Josh,' Nat suggested. 'Maybe he could put the wham back into your bam?'

'That's right, have a laugh about it.'

'I'm serious, man. You can't lose much, can you? Only your dignity, and I think you've lost that already.'

We shut up pretty quick after that cause the girls appeared. Every time Miz and Sal showed up they brought more mates with them. I don't know how they did it, but the women were starting to outnumber the rest of us.

Eleventh Bit

Funky moped

The other lads steadily appeared, then Josh came back, hood up and new shades clamped around his head.

Jude went straight to him and started on about his bike. It was a real beauty, parked by the kerb in full sunlight to show off the gleaming chrome and shapely black body. Mirrors shot out from the thing at all angles like thunderbolts. However, the bike may have been standing there in all its splendour but Jude was wilting by the minute.

'I'm not riding in on the BMW, Jude. I'm not. Now listen. You ride it to Truro, we'll meet you there at the station. And you can escort me in.'

Jude brightened. 'Me ride it?'

'Of course, on my right-hand side.'

At which point Jack and Jimmy closed in.

'Wait a minute wait a minute, we should be on your right and left.'

This started a right old argument about who should be where and what the pecking order was; incredibly, Jack and Jimmy had a tight cast list worked out. Where was I? Oh, you know, somewhere down the bottom, third extra on the left. Little more than a walk-on part. I didn't care – at least, that's what I told 'em. In no uncertain terms. Sal dragged me away from the fray.

'What are you like? Stop it! Let 'em argue – it means nothing. It's a waste of time.'

I glanced back at Jimmy and Jack, cool as ever, not a blond hair out of place. Si and Andy, on the other hand, were going at it hammer and tongs, looking like a couple of stand-ins for Animal off *The Muppets*.

'What's happened to you this week?' Sal said to me. 'You seem different. Why didn't you call?'

I kicked at the kerb and sighed a lot. 'I can't get my head around what happened to you,' I said eventually.

'Well, don't try – just accept it. It was a miracle.'

'But that's that I mean. What's a miracle? I just wanna blank it out – just make like it never happened. You never got sick and you never got better . . .'

'OK, then.'

'What?'

'Pretend it never happened.'

'But I can't do that. You've lived through something.'

'Yea, but it's my life not yours. If worrying about it turns you into Woody Allen, then forget it. Turn back time and let's just carry on. Life's too short.'

'Apparently not – cause you can make it last longer if you want.'

She looked at me like I was mad.

Josh shut everyone up at that moment.

'Jack, Jimmy, shut up and listen. I don't care where you think you should be; pecking orders are for chickens. If you want to be top dog, then get with the broken and the rejected. But as for today – here's the deal. Jimmy, when we get to Truro, you'll find a Honda garage two streets away from the station. Out the exit and keep walking left. There's a little yellow 50 c.c. moped on the forecourt. You'll find a tall guy with glasses and black hair. His name's Dan. Tell him Josh is ready for it and he'll let you ride away on it.'

'What?'

'It's all right. I've arranged it.'

'I don't mean that – I mean I'm not being seen dead on a little yellow Honda.'

Josh let out an exasperated, guttural yell. 'Just do it!' he snapped.

And no one said anything else.

Two miles an hour

'You're not going to believe this . . .'

It was unbelievable. I don't know if Jude had phoned ahead and promised free beer. Maybe news had spread about Josh's ability to produce magic burgers. Whatever, the streets of Truro were jammed with people who were clearly not there for a trip to Argos. There was a massive banner hanging over the main street, and kids wearing baseball caps and T-shirts sporting his name. People had gone up onto the roofs of offices and shops; teenagers had shinned up traffic lights and there were OAPs sitting on balconies and aboard open-topped buses. And all of them chanting: 'Josh! Josh! Josh! Josh!'

Ridiculous. They didn't know him. They'd just heard rumours and seen TV shows. Josh wasn't bothered; he was in his element, sitting astride his little Honda, wearing a grin bigger than the moped.

Jude was doing his best to look in control on that massive bike of his but it was hard for him to stay upright going at two miles per hour. I sidled up to him as he tottered like Goliath on stilts.

'Is this your doing?' I asked.

Despite his discomfort, he grinned and winked. 'A few calls, Tom. A radio station here, newspaper there. A couple of ads on the internet. I just reeled in a few favours. Anyway, who loses? The shops and bars will make a killing. It's great publicity for all of us.'

'Josh! Josh! Josh! Josh!'

It made me wonder whether going through London might have not been easier.

We crawled through the waves of people, it was like we'd won the World Cup or something. They threw flowers, confetti, money, loo rolls. It was truly overwhelming.

We came to another standstill as a local Boy's Brigade band came crossing the road. I saw Jude pull up alongside Josh.

'Now's the time, Josh,' he yelled above the noise. 'You got them eating out of your hand.' And he pulled a small megaphone from the gleaming box behind his saddle.

Josh just smiled and nodded. But he didn't take the megaphone.

'What you waiting for?' Jude urged. 'Address the people. Start something big.'

Josh was still smiling but this time he shook his head. 'First rule of fame, Jude – never believe what the crowd tells you. They'll say anything to get your attention cause they want a part of you. It's not that they don't mean what they say, they do – right here, right now. But it's like rice planted on scree slopes – it doesn't last. They'll go home when the shows over, make a cup of tea and a bacon sandwich and by tomorrow they'll have changed their mind.'

Jude's face clouded over. 'Don't say that, that's defeatist talk,' he said.

'No, it's real life, Jude.'

Jude kicked at the ground, lost his footing and he and the massive BMW toppled over.

The Boy's Brigade moved on and so did Josh. I ran to help Jude up.

'Get off!' he snapped, and he threw a fist in my direction.

An hour later we crawled into the cathedral grounds. Thousands of us. The place was a wall of bodies. Cathedral staff began pouring out of every doorway.

'What's going on?' one of them asked. 'They can't stay here.'

'They're with me,' Josh said.

'Who are they?' demanded a small official with a huge moustache.

'People. Black, white, rich, poor, straight, gay. Just people.'

'Well, they can't come here.'

'Too late.'

The Boy's Brigade had struck up again and somewhere an electric guitar was banging out 'Knocking on Heaven's Door'. A mobile disco was just rolling up and ice cream vans and hot dog trailers were doing a roaring trade. Another cathedral official came over.

'You gotta shut them up,' he shouted. 'We have a service of reverence going on in there.'

'We have one going on out here,' Josh called back and he held out his hand. 'I'm Josh.'

'So? You can't just march in here and fill the place with rowdy tourists.'

'They're not tourists, they're people, and we'll never stop them. You may as well bring your people out and join in the party.'

'Worship is not a party.'

'Really – why not? D'you have nothing to celebrate?'

'I don't have time for this. The Dean'll be here soon.'

'Then the party'll be complete. Come on, lighten up. This isn't going away. You may plan your nice neat services inside but the worship out here will still happen and ragged life will flourish beyond the safe parameters.'

The officials shook their heads. Josh looked at me.

'Bring any sandwiches?' he asked.

'I got a couple left over that I bought on the train,' I said.

He grimaced. 'We can't multiply those, there'll be a riot. See that kid with the fish and chips? Call him over.'

After that it was like déjà vu. He fed the people – or rather, he took the kids' dinner and told us to feed 'em. Then he went inside the cathedral and threw a wobbly. He really didn't seem to like the barriers and the atmosphere that kept people at bay.

I went looking for Sal. She and Miz had slipped off to buy something somewhere. And that's when I bumped into Jude.

'Wow! Where you been? I asked. 'You missed the fun at the cathedral. I thought you were going to video it?'

He looked flustered. 'Oh, I had a few things to do,' he said. 'I gotta keep moving.'

And he slipped away down a side alley.

I glanced up at the sandstone building he'd just come from. It was the local police station. Odd.

Something made me leg it back to the cathedral, and sure enough, the Bill were just hacking their way through the crowd. They cut a path and flooded into the building. I had to battle to get through the crowd myself and, by the time I got there, the police were accusing Si and Andy and the others of something or other. There was no sign of Josh.

'Where's Josh?' I asked.

'He slipped out the back,' muttered Jack. 'He saw this coming and figured it was time to make a hasty exit. We said we'd cover him. Where were you?'

'Oh, just hanging around,' I said.

We got off lightly with a caution and a bill for the damage, which fortunately wasn't as bad as the last time. The crowds slowly dispersed and we sauntered back to the train station. We met Miz and Sal and Jo on the way.

'Josh's gone back home,' Miz said. 'He said something about it being safer that way.'

I didn't bump into Jude again. He must have figured the same thing.

A chemical weapon waiting to go off

We didn't see Josh again for a couple of days, then word got around that he was going to be at Si's on Monday night. There was a match on TV so we crammed into Si's front room to watch Liverpool v. Arsenal. Si really did have a wife, and three kids. And a mortgage and a garden shed and a greenhouse. He just didn't look the type. He also loved Arsenal. Which was bad news for him because we didn't. Jack and Jimmy had just got back with the beer and the cheeseburgers. The opening whistle blew, Arsenal scored, two players got sent off, Si and Jimmy came to blows and a minute later there was a knock on the door.

'Who's that?'

'Miz, you get it,' said Jack.

'I don't think so,' said Miz.

Just then Mark, Si's five-year-old, appeared in the doorway.

'Dad, I can't sleep . . .'

Miz scooped him up. 'Hey, Superman, I hear you got a new bed with tractors all over it . . .' She turned him upside down and carried him back upstairs. The knocking at the door grew louder, more insistent.

'Hey, dudes, someone get that,' said Nat.

'Yea, and another beer while you're up,' said Jimmy.

Josh got up. He came back with Mr Keats and the cartoon baddies.

'Get out of my house,' said Si quietly, almost under his breath.

'All in good time,' said Keats. 'Don't want to spoil the party. Liverpool winning yet?'

No one told him.

'Whatever,' he said with a shrug.

'What do you want, Mr Keats?' Josh asked him. 'I don't want to hurry you but this is time out for us, a bit of R and R, you know.'

Keats settled his shoulders, squared up to Josh and started in.

'I want you to heal my boy. He's a drug addict. He's in hospital after an overdose, he's an idiot, the doctors say he's knocking on heaven's door. You can fix him. I want you to do it and I want you to take away his addiction.'

Josh gave a half-smile and was about to reply.

'What you smiling for? Didn't you hear? He's in a bad way and he's my son. Get him off death's doorstep and do it now. I can make it worth your while. I know you can do it. I know how it works. Look at the league of gentlemen here.' He wagged a thumb at Wallace and Gromit. 'I tell 'em jump and they jump. That's how it goes. So tell this son of mine to shape up and sort out his life. Do what you do best. Work a miracle or whatever you call it.'

Josh shook his head. 'I need some time on this one.'

'We don't have time, didn't you hear? He's bangin' on death's door.'

Josh cleared his throat. 'Give me your card,' he said.

'What?'

'Your business card, Mr Keats. That's all I need. Trust me.'

Keats fumbled in his overcoat and proffered a gold-etched wafer. Josh took it, glanced at it and nodded. 'I'll be in touch,' he said.

'You'd better do more than that,' Keats said. 'Or it won't just be the kid who's heading for the morgue.' And he nodded to his minders and left.

Josh heaved a sigh of relief. 'Well I didn't see that one coming,' he said.

'I wouldn't mess with him,' Jack said. 'He's a chemical weapon waiting to go off.'

And Arsenal scored again.

Lasered on red-blooded hearts

During half time, Josh's phone rang. He didn't recognise the number so he handed it to Jack.

'Hello? Yea? How d'you get this number? How? Is this a wind-up? Well, what do you want?'

Jack listened then lowered the phone.

'Believe it or not it's the prime minister's private secretary. Are you bovvered?'

Josh rolled his eyes and said, 'Yea, I'm bovvered,' and he stood up and took the phone.

'Hello? Speaking. Sure, I'm coming. Yea, looking forward to it . . . I think . . . Will I what? Of course not. I can't endorse that. I'll say what seems most effective . . . No. You know that's not my agenda . . . No. I won't. Of course not. I can't back that kind of notion, either. Let him fight his own battles. Because it's not who I am, it's not . . . it's not what I'm there for. I'll take that risk. Am I? What is power – the ability to give it up? They're saying what? Well, many people may say many things, Private

Secretary, words come easy. Really? What's truth? You tell me. Is it relative? What was it Lennon said – life is what happens while you're making plans. Well, maybe truth is what happens while you're making claims. I'm running out of time but . . . yes . . . wait a minute, please! Let me finish. You'll know what I stand for and what my intentions are when you see my . . . what do you call it . . . manifesto. No, it's not printed on paper, it's lasered on red-blooded hearts. Sure you can have a copy – you can be a copy in fact. Dangerous? To whom? Listen – I'm not fighting this battle with you any more. My final answer is no. NO! I'll be there on Friday but I won't play your games. Goodnight.' And he hung up.

'I'm in trouble,' he said. 'I won't join their posse.'

Jack passed him a beer.

'It's hard for people,' Josh went on. 'They hear so many different things. The media holds the world in the palm of its hand. I'm not sure which is worse, a big fat lie or a little filtered truth. There's spin everywhere – photos are airbrushed, voices manipulated, people mis-represented, situations distorted. But one day reality will be broadcast properly – with no magic CGI. It'll be projected on the screens of the sky and everyone will see what really takes place.'

Josh looked at our faces. We were like the alternative seven dwarves – cool, confused, nonchalant, scared, frustrated, angry and sarcastic.

'One day the bull will be hosed away, just be ready for it. It's all you can be. You won't know when it's gonna happen, though for many people second-guessing the moment will be a full-time occupation. But you won't predict it. In the same way that you can't imagine a new colour. It's beyond the capacity of human thought.'

He suddenly dropped to the sofa and clamped his hands to his temples.

'You OK?' said Miz. 'You look terrible.'

'I've been getting bad headaches lately,' he said. 'Too much stress . . . too much caffeine and junk food . . .'

'Too many people asking you for too much. Take these.' Miz grabbed her bag and fished out some pills. She felt his forehead. 'I'll get you a glass of water,' she said. 'Sit quiet for a while.'

But he wouldn't.

'The only thing that really matters about the end of everything is logging its possibility. It'll be like ten people queuing for a football match and then, just as the gates are about to open, five of them realise they left their tickets at home. In the time it takes them to travel home and back, the game starts and they miss the deciding goal.'

Miz came back with a bottle of water and a damp cloth. She broke the seal and put the water to his lips. Then she held the cloth to his forehead.

'You need a break,' she said softly. 'This kind of life'll kill you.'

'Too right,' he said. 'Where was I?'

'I think you'd finished,' she said firmly.

'Nearly. Many people will come along claiming to have the answer or, worse still, to be the answer. So test everything. Believe nothing till you've tested it. But do test it. To believe nothing because you haven't tested anything is stupid. And you don't wanna be stupid. Legitimate software is virus free. Good cars run smoothly. You know what I'm saying. Don't be naïve . . . Boy, I'm tired. Too many late nights.' He lay back on the sofa and closed his eyes. Miz kept stroking his forehead. We all looked at each other. It seemed like a good moment to leave but no one was going anywhere. He opened one eye and cracked a smile.

'It's OK, guys,' he said. 'Sermon over.'

Miz gave him some sleeping pills and he said he'd crash out there at Si's. Arsenal scored a third goal but we missed that.

Doughnuts

We met again in the clearing three days later, Thursday night. Sal was there. And Si, and Jack and Jimmy and Nat, and Miz, all of them. The sky was clear and the evening was the last good one of that summer. We sat around on stumps and rocks and Josh produced pizza, doughnuts, Coke and coffee. Josh did all the work. He poured the drinks and paper-plated the food. Then he passed it round.

'I always want you to remember this night,' he said, and suddenly I felt my chest start to tighten. I sniffed and rubbed my left eye. 'This is the beginning of something, and all birth is painful.'

He held up one of the doughnuts and ripped it in two. The bright red jam dripped across his hands.

'Let this remind you, think of it as my lifeblood and my body. When you see me broken, remember tonight and this broken food. Keep doing this together. Meet, share food, remember me.'

I felt as if I couldn't breathe, my chest was going to explode.

'I've told you lots of things – hopefully, between you, you'll recall them later. Now I'm gonna go away – to the summit, yes – but further, and you know why, and you know where . . .'

'We don't!'

They all looked at me. I knew I had tears streaming down my face and I knew I looked a fool but I couldn't hold it back.

'What's gonna happen? Promise us it'll be OK.'

He nodded, and at the same time I felt Sal's hand on my arm.

'It will be OK. I'm going to sort things out for you guys, and not just you, everyone who comes after you. I'm going to do the hardest work of my life, and when it's done you'll have a future and the kind of hope that lasts forever.'

'How can we find it, though?'

'In me. This isn't the end of the journey, it's just the beginning. I'm the way, keep following me.'

Nat raised a finger. 'Josh, dude, can you just like, give us a bit of evidence? I mean, I'm starting to get the scenario, sort of see it, but not crystal. Can you, like – prove any of this, dude? Can you prove it's, like – real? Only I'm totalled by it all, know what I mean, dude?'

Josh shook his head and smacked a hand to his forehead.

'Nat, how long has this been going on? Just trust me on this. I'm God's hands and feet to you. I'm his body. This is the proof you get. If you can't trust that then at least think on the things I've done. Look at Sal, for goodness' sake. Alive and well!'

'But you need to show the world, they need to see you. Now. Before it's too late.'

'No, Jude – you need to show the world. All of you. When I'm gone, you'll be the hands and feet of God, you'll be his smile, and his face, you'll be his arms and his muscles. That's why I'm going – because you can go all over the world, and you won't be alone. I'll be with you all the time. You look so scared, you guys! Calm down, don't worry. It'll make sense.'

We finished up the doughnuts and sat for a long time in the dark. We didn't want the night to end. A lot of the group had dozed off when Jude got up.

'Where you going?' Si asked.

'Away,' he said. 'I got things to do.'

We stared after him as he slipped into the shadows, his black coat sweeping behind him as he went.

'Betrayal, denial, it's all gonna happen tonight.' Josh said this almost in a trance.

'Don't be stupid,' said Si. 'Course it won't.'

'Then come with me to London. I need your support.'

'Fine, I will.'

'Me too,' said Jack and Miz nodded with him.

'Tom?'

I looked at Sal; she was sleeping peacefully beside me. I looked at her hand clutching my arm. I couldn't go.

'I'm sorry,' I said.

Josh leant over and pressed his head against mine. 'It's OK,' he said. 'I understand. Let go of Mike. Be yourself. One day at a time. You can do it.'

And he was gone. Just like my twin.

Nothing's all right

But not for long. Seconds later and they were back. I'd just settled down next to Sal when there was a rush of breaking twigs and the scuffling of feet backing up through undergrowth. Si, Josh, Jack and Miz reversed back into the clearing with Keats and his entourage of cartoon baddies forcing them backwards.

'What the . . .'

It was Jimmy. He was standing up, and Andy too. They were ready for a fight.

'Nobody be stupid,' said Keats. 'We've just come for a little chat.'

Keats reached inside his black overcoat and pulled a gun. He did it with exaggerated flare, as if he was pulling a rabbit from his sleeve.

'You killed my son.'

'What?' said Josh.

'You heard. I asked you to sort him out and you wouldn't do it. He died yesterday. What you gonna do about it?'

'Nothing, I . . .'

'I wouldn't say that if I were you.' His hand shook as he levelled the gun at Josh's face.

'Now, heal my son.'

'What?'

'HEAL MY SON! Bring him back! NOW!' Keats jammed the barrel of his gun right into Josh's forehead. 'Do it now!'

'This is crazy!'

We were all awake by this time and on our feet. Wallace and Gromit pulled pistols and were waving them in our general direction. They had to keep circling as we were dotted all over the clearing. You could hear everyone's breathing coming shallow and fast.

'It doesn't work like this,' Josh said.

'Make him live or you die!'

At which point a gun went off and we all recoiled, grabbing our bodies as we fell. I looked at my chest but it was dry, so I scoured the clearing, half expecting Sal to be lying in a pool of her own blood. But there was nothing. Jack, Jimmy, Nat, Miz, all of us, we were on the ground intact, staring at everyone else. All except Si. He was standing up with a plume of smoke rising from his fingers. Well, not his fingers. The gun in his fingers.

'That's mine!' yelled Nat, and forgetting the situation he shot up and tried to wrestle the old revolver from Si's hands. It wasn't difficult, Si let it go immediately. He was more preoccupied with the ground ahead of him, and the body sprawled across the fallen tree.

'You've killed him!' shouted Keats.

One of Keats' minders was sprayed across the trunk, a fountain of blood cascading from his neck.

'You shot Gromit!' said Nat, nursing his gun.

'What?' boomed Keats. 'Who's Gromit?' He stumbled over and kicked at the body.

Josh pushed Keats aside and knelt down in the dirt.

'Someone got a rag?' he asked.

Miz pulled a scarf from her bag and threw it to him. Josh clamped it against the wound.

'What are you doing?' Keats thundered, his voice on permanent loud.

But Josh said nothing. He just kept stifling the wound and staring at the man's bleached face. The clearing fell silent. No one could think of the next move. I was about to say something stupid when there was an almighty gasp from the guy on the ground. He twitched and coughed and shot up into a sitting position. Josh fell back onto his haunches.

'What the . . .'

The scarf fell away from the wound. It was still soaked in fresh blood, but the guy's neck was clean.

'But . . . I thought you just . . . Where'd all that blood come from?' It was Keats, his mouth flapping like a glove puppet.

'He's all right,' said Josh, standing and offering the minder his hand. 'Come on, get up. It's over.'

Gromit staggered up and kept patting his neck with his hand. There really was nothing left of the bullet wound.

'Er . . . what now?' Wallace asked, having, I guess, never encountered this kind of thing before.

Keats was lost for a moment.

'He'll be all right,' said Josh. 'Now give us a break.'

Keats suddenly regrouped.

'But what about my boy?' he said, his face twisted like a ruined painting.

Josh looked at him for the longest time.

'I was talking about your boy,' he said eventually.

Keats' expression fell. 'You mean . . .'

'I guess faith comes in all kinds of guises, Mr Keats. I just never witnessed it through the barrel of a gun before. Please go.'

Keats nodded weakly. 'Well . . . if you say everything's all right.'

'Believe me, everything's not all right. Nothing's all right. But your boy will live.'

We watched them leave in a bewildered silence. Then Nat turned on Si.

'You nicked my gun, dude!'

'I thought I might need it. Got a problem with that?'

'Yes!' Now Nat levelled the barrel at Si's head.

'Oh, for goodness' sake!' said Josh. 'Grow up! At least act your shoe size if you can't manage your age.'

'What's that mean?'

'It means give me the gun.'

Nat slowly handed it to Josh. Josh snatched it and flung it in the bushes.

'Some kid'll find that,' said Nat.

'No they won't.'

Nat leapt into the undergrowth and crashed about.

'You won't find it,' said Josh. 'For once in my life I've come close to doing a magic trick. It's gone.' He looked at the rest of us. 'Come on, you can't stay here now. We'd better get out of here before the police show up wondering what all the noise was about.'

As Josh ploughed through the undergrowth, thorns clawed at his clothes and tore the flesh on his arms. He turned and shouted at the bushes and I swear I saw the branches recoil under the power of his verbal assault.

Twelfth Bit

Strangers on a train

'Where are we going?'

We had walked for a good twenty minutes, it was well dark now.

'The railway station.'

'Why?'

Josh turned wearily. 'I'm going to London. I want you guys to come with me. But it's up to you.' And he started walking again.

'I don't understand it. You don't need to go to this summit. You said you wouldn't play their games.'

'I have to go. Call it a date with destiny.'

We looked at each other. Sal said, 'I'm going.'

So I knew then that I was going too. We all knew.

Once on board we split up. No idea why. We didn't plan it, he didn't suggest it. We just acted like we didn't know one another. It was like a scene from *The Great Escape*. Sal and I stood in the section between two coaches, staring out of the window. The night was so black we couldn't see a thing out there, which was somehow the perfect metaphor. There was an ominous feeling about everything.

Two women in their twenties came towards us out of one of the carriages.

'Sal! What you doing here?'

'Oh, just going to London,' she said, and as she announced it, I suddenly realised none of us had brought bags or coats or anything useful.

'London, why?'

Sal glanced at me. 'Oh, Tom, these are two mates I used to go to college with,' she said. 'Paula and Bex.'

I nodded at them and looked away, but not soon enough to miss the one called Bex mouthing the word *boyfriend* in a questioning manner. I didn't see Sal's response.

'We're trying to track down the new big thing,' I heard one of them say.

'What's that?' asked Sal.

'Oh, come on, don't tell us you don't know. Mr Miracle. The Cool Medicine Man. Bex is on a mission to get to the real Josh Churchill.'

Now, which way's *this* gonna go, I thought. I was being no use at all. I looked about, but sadly there were no holes opening up in the floor. We were cornered. I was waiting for Sal to say something non-committal but nothing was coming out.

'Oh, come on! You've heard of the guy. He's been in all the papers. They reckon he can do anything, walk on water, conjure up electric storms, turn Coke into Bacardi. Might even be able to find Paula a bloke that doesn't sleep around.'

They laughed. Sal joined in. 'I know who you mean,' she said, 'but why are you asking us?'

'We're not asking you. No need to be all defensive, girl. We're telling you. Come with us. Help us find him. He's in London this weekend.'

'No thanks. We got our own agenda planned,' she said, and I guessed she raised her eyebrows, cause there was a dirty laugh from the others. I glanced back.

'You'll regret it,' said Paula, winking at me.

'No, she won't,' said Bex with another laugh.

They said a few more things and then wandered off looking for a seat.

Sal and I looked at each other for a long time. We both knew we'd been covering for Josh but somehow it still felt like a betrayal.

After a couple of changes we pulled in at Paddington and flooded out of the train. It was 2 a.m. but the place was still awash with travellers. The gaggle of cosmopolitan accents was like listening to the Eurovision Song Contest. We regrouped outside McDonald's and viewed each other with bleary eyes. Si put a hand on Josh's shoulder.

'I don't know what the hell we're doing here,' he said. 'We can't come with you to the summit like a bunch of groupies.'

'Yea, we can,' said Jimmy. 'We can go as minders.'

Andy glanced round. 'Sure. Jack, Jimmy and Si could carry it off, maybe even Nat . . . but not the rest of us.'

'Anyone seen Jude?' Josh asked.

'Not since he left the clearing. There's something up with that guy. He's been acting strange.'

'That's nothing new,' said Miz. 'He's always given me the creeps.'

'OK, OK, let's ease off the pedal a bit. I'm not sure they'll let me bring an entourage but it may be worth a try. You four come with me like Andy suggested. I'm gonna call the hotel. The rest of you call this number. It's a student hostel. Just round the corner. I know the guys there, they're American and make great pie. They'll put you up for the night. I'll make contact in the morning.'

He motioned to Jack and the others and the guys followed him. Andy pulled out his mobile and dialled the number.

It's strange how normal cataclysmic moments can often be. No climactic music, no slow-mo farewell, no meaningful exchanges or classic one-liners. Just a wave of the hand and a brief smile. Maybe Josh was the only one who could sense the tremors as the world began shifting on its axis.

Guy Fawkes

We slept late, and woke to find the hostel proprietors had left us food in the huge Victorian dining room. Including pie. Matt discovered a lounge next door with a widescreen TV so we grabbed a mountain of eggy bread and three pots of coffee and lay about on beanbags and weary sofas waiting to catch coverage of the summit. A bomb had gone off in India so Sky News was stuffed with eyewitness reports. A hundred and fifty dead, at least.

'Shouldn't they have made contact now?' Andy said, eyeing his watch.

It was 10.45.

'He'll call when he's ready,' said Matt. 'Hey! Have you seen what's on the other side on the Discovery Channel? *The Secret Life of Bed Bugs.*'

We hadn't and didn't care.

'Don't change the channel,' Miz said.

A criminally happy presenter appeared on the screen and announced the cameras were finally going over to the summit. The usual shots of limos and black-coated MPs flashed on the screen.

'What the . . .' I sat up and stared, mouth sagging open.

Ticker taping along the bottom there was news of another attempted bombing. This time in London. A number of suspects had been picked up in the early hours and detained. No further information yet available.

'D'you think someone's after the summit?' Miz said.

'Yea, Guy Fawkes,' said Matt.

'Please – not another terrorist plot,' said Sal.

And suddenly there it was. The bare facts. Five men apprehended in a Kensington hotel. Found in possession of detonators and explosives in a raid in the early hours. Early indications suggest they were on their way to the summit.

'History repeats itself!' said Matt. 'It really is November fifth.'

Five minutes went by. The same report passed along the bottom of the screen six times.

Andy checked his phone again. No messages, no texts, nothing.

'He'll be fine,' said Matt.

Andy tried calling Si but his phone was off. Jack and Jimmy's too. No one knew Nat's number.

'Try Jude,' I said suddenly.

Andy knew that one. He dialled, we muted the TV and we waited.

'Jude, hey! Where are you? What d'you mean? Heard what? Oh yea, we got it on now. What? Where are you? Are you sure? Don't do anything stupid! Us? We're at Mansion Heights, it's a hostel round the corner from Paddington.'

'What's going on?' I asked him.

Andy folded his phone and stared at me. 'Those five guys they picked up . . .'

'No! You're kidding!' I said, but he nodded.

'What?' said Matt. 'Stop talking in riddles. You're worse than Josh.'

'We're talking about Josh.'

And even as the truth sank in, their faces flashed up on the screen.

'Turn up the sound!' Matt shouted and he threw himself at the remote.

'The five missing men have been named by police. They are . . .'

'Missing?' Miz said.

'Shut up!'

The ticker tape along the bottom informed the world that Josh and the others had been picked up, held in cells overnight and were being transported to another station when a gang of armed men ambushed the prison truck and busted them out. The police claimed a gang of at least ten men had taken the suspects away in two cars less than thirty minutes ago.

'This is not happening!' said Andy.

'I don't believe any of this,' said Matt. 'It's like something out of *24*.'

'Shut up. Look, they've got my brother.' Andy suddenly snapped his fingers. 'Keats!' he yelled. 'It's bloody Keats. He's gonna kill 'em all.'

'Slow down,' said Sal. 'Don't be stupid. Josh gave Keats what he wanted, remember?'

'So he claimed. But how do we know?' Andy shook his head. 'Maybe his son never resuscitated, maybe Josh couldn't bring him back. It's Keats, I know it. He planted the explosives and waited for the cops to get them and then sprung them so he could get his revenge.'

'That doesn't add up, might as well just spring 'em in the first place. Why bother planting the explosives?' Matt said. 'No, my money's on the government. I bet they planted the explosives to discredit Josh.'

'The Prime Minister? Don't be stupid. This isn't Zimbabwe,' said Andy, 'or America.'

'I think it all stinks,' said Miz. 'It's one big cover story.'

The arguing grew wings and took flight; all kinds of theories vied for supremacy.

I'd had enough. This wasn't part of the plan. Josh was invincible. This just couldn't be happening. A guy who brings your girlfriend back to life doesn't get arrested for terrorism.

I strolled outside and sat on the steps. Outside people were doing what they always did, oblivious to the madness being played out in their own city. It calmed me a little. I heard a footstep behind me. I knew it was Sal. It had to be.

'This just isn't happening,' I said.

'You're telling me.'

It was Jude. He looked terrible. Eyes like cracked marbles, a bruise on his left cheek and his clothes covered in dirt.

'What's going on? What happened to you?'

'I'm gonna sort it,' he said. 'I did something stupid but I can fix it.' He squinted at me; his left eye was starting to swell and close. 'Come with me, Tom. I need your support. You're the only one of these guys I trust. You're a rock for me, mate.'

Backstreets and lock-ups

I don't know why I went. I'm useless in a crisis. Jude could be persuasive I guess, especially when he was desperate. He wouldn't even let me go back and tell the others. I'm a bad judge of character.

'We have to walk,' he said, limping along. 'The tube has cameras.'

'How d'you get beaten up like this?'

'Long story. Tried to right a wrong and ended up doing more damage.'

'It's Keats isn't it? He's gonna kill Josh.'

Jude stopped dead, turned and for the first time he smiled.

'You're kidding me,' he said and he laughed then winced and held his ribs. 'You don't think some lowlife like Keats has the power to do this, do you?'

'You told me he was violent. Told me he was a nasty piece of work.'

'In Cornwall. This is the big apple, mate. They never heard of Keats down here – they'd have him for breakfast and then eat a fry-up.'

'Then I don't get it.'

'You will,' said Jude and he slapped me on the shoulder and moved off again. 'Keats,' I heard him mutter as we went and he started chuckling to himself again.

We ended up in a dismal backstreet pub. Jude went straight to the bar and had a side-of-the-mouth conversation with the barman. Everybody else in the place had a dog and massive Iron Maiden tattoos. Jude actually fitted in well with his spattered coat and purple bruising. I did my best not to make eye contact with man or beast.

'What are we doing here?' I hissed when he'd finished necking with the barman.

'Believe it or not, the barman knows where Josh is. He's a casual member of the gang that sprung him.'

'How d'you know him?'

'Keep your voice down. I know lots of things. I do plenty of favours for people so I can call 'em in. He's gone to get his girlfriend so she can take us for a walk.'

A girl in ripped black clothes appeared and introduced herself as Siouxsie, 'as in Siouxsie and the Banshees'. She was buried under ten layers of make-up and must have been all of fifteen.

'You're looking for your mate?' she asked, lighting a cigarette.

We nodded. She sniffed and adjusted an exposed bra strap.

'Come on,' she said. 'I'll take ya.'

I couldn't make it add up in my head. What did this dimly lit backstreet pub in London have to do with Josh from sleepy Cornwall? When did these two worlds collide?

Siouxsie clicked up the steps in her high-heeled boots and led us back out into the streets. I started to ask questions but Jude just looked at me and shook his head. I shut up.

She led us across more backstreets and finally to a line of lock-ups under a bridge. She looked at Jude and rubbed her fingers. Jude pulled a wad of notes from his pocket and handed them over.

'Number five,' she said. 'Good luck.'

And she knocked on a nearby door three times and walked away.

Curtains

The door fell open and an old guy in odd slippers, with broken glasses, a wispy beard and bow legs looked out. Surely this wasn't the mastermind behind the abduction of the saviour of the planet. We went in and my eyes adjusted to the gas lamps in there.

The place was done out like Aladdin's cave. It was like the *Antiques Roadshow*. Grandfather clocks, bedpans, mangles, sewing machines, gramophones, even the funnel from an old steam engine.

'I want to talk to them,' Jude said, no introductions, no handshakes.

'You can't,' the old guy rasped, his voice like an old rotavator.

'But I have to – I have to explain, I have to get them out of there.'

'It's too late.'

'Too late?'

A deathly silence fell over the lock-up. Three grandfather clocks ticked and groaned in the background.

'They're dead?' I asked and the old man laughed, then coughed asthmatically for a long time.

'Dead? No, they done a runner,' he said when he'd got his breath back.

'They escaped?'

'No. They didn't want 'em, they only wanted him, so we offered them a deal and they took it.'

'They did a deal?'

'Yea. Cup o' tea? Drop o' whisky?'

'What about Josh?'

'Oh no, we still got the main man. But you're wastin' your time there. No amount of wheelin' and dealin' is gonna get him out. It's curtains for the boy, poor devil.'

'I have money, I can pay.'

'Should have thought of that earlier. Too late now. You set him up perfectly and we paid you good. Don't complain.'

I turned on Jude. 'You set him up?'

'I'll explain later. Shut up, Tom, this is my show.'

'No, it's not,' said the old guy, 'it ain't any of our shows. It's theirs now. Nothing you can do. Money or no money. You sure you won't have that whisky?'

We walked back in silence. When we got to the nearest tube, Jude slowed down.

'I'm going underground,' he said.

'But you've told me nothing, and I thought you said there were cameras down there.'

'I don't give a monkey's.'

'Wait! What happened? I mean – how d'you get so beat up?'

Jude sniffed and squinted at me, the bruise on his left cheek was turning an ever darker shade of purple.

'It's all my fault, Tom. The old guy was telling the truth – I set Josh up, cause I thought it would provoke him into a showdown. Hell, can't you see it? Can't anyone see it? He has the power to change everything.' Jude's cheeks flushed a dark red. 'He has the means and the ability to kick out the self-serving monsters that rule this country. He cares about what really matters, but he won't stand up to them and show them how powerful he is. I don't get it. I thought I could make him do that. I tried, I really tried, but it went so wrong. I followed them to argue with them – that's when I got the beating. The thugs that took him down laid into me.' He smiled at me one last time and raised a bloodstained hand. The nails were splintered and one of them was skewed and hanging loose.

'See ya, Tom.' And he disappeared down the steps into the station, tripping over his feet as he went.

Now, I've never been good at directions, and remembering the route that Siouxsie had brought us was never going to happen for me.

I went round in circles getting more and more angry, more and more lost. I didn't want to call the others because, well, the same reason it takes a million male sperm to fertilise one egg – I didn't want to ask for directions.

I don't like the underground, I'm claustrophobic, but eventually it was that or phone a friend and look an idiot. So I ducked down the nearest stairwell, found a map, tried to read it, asked a passer-by and eventually worked out the route back to the hostel. The platform down there was wall-to-wall bodies. Some hold-up on the line had grounded the trains. I had to wait half an hour. It was way past lunchtime now, not that I was hungry.

I took the trains and made the connections back to the hostel in a daze. I just wanted to run away, back to Cornwall, back to what I knew. Something safe and familiar. I just wanted to switch on Sky Scandinavian Three, crack open a Guinness and feel sorry for myself.

But I couldn't do that. I had Sal to worry about now.

Not our finest hour

What I didn't expect to find when I got back was Si and Jimmy sitting on the step.

'Tom!' they called. 'We need you.'

Everybody needed me today.

'We can't get in, mate, what's the door code?'

I looked at their faces. There wasn't a scratch on either of them.

'You cut a deal, didn't you?' I said.

They glanced at one another.

'Don't start. You weren't there, Tom,' said Si.

'Let us in,' Jimmy said. 'We'll explain inside.'

'Where's Jack and Nat?'

They shrugged. 'We don't know. We think Nat may have got picked up again by the Bill and Jack doubled back.'

I let them in and led them to the lounge. The others were still there watching TV amongst a growing pile of beer cans and dirty plates.

'Look at this mess,' I complained.

'Where've you been?' Sal asked, and she came over and smacked me. 'You scared me stupid.'

And she hit me again. Hard.

'It was Jude. I'll explain.'

I told them what I knew. It didn't really amount to much. Si added more.

'Jude set this up,' he said. 'He planted the detonators and explosives.'

'You're kidding! How'd he get explosives?'

'He knows a lot of people,' he said.

I thought of the day I'd seen him on the seafront with a FedEx parcel under his arm.

'I reckon the idiot was trying to spark some kind of revolution,' Jimmy said. He looked at Si. 'We'd better tell 'em what happened. When we got to the hotel we'd not been there ten minutes when there was a knock at the door. It was the cops. They waltzed in, flashed a bit of paper and started searching the room. It was a set-up. Totally. We'd not brought anything yet they found all this stuff. Josh told me later Jude knew where we were going to stay. I reckon he was hanging around in the shadows when they bundled us into the car. The cops took us away and locked us up. Next morning we were on our way in a van when there was a gunshot and one of the tyres blew. The truck went into a skid, we were thrown about like Muppets in the back. Next thing you know there's another bang and the doors flew open. A bunch of guys in balaclavas hauled us out, put bags on our heads and threw us in a couple of cars. When the cars stopped we were dragged out and bundled into this lock-up. Place looked like an antiques emporium.'

'I've been there,' I said. 'And so has Jude.'

'That proves it, then. An old guy gave us tea and whisky and some stale sandwiches and we waited. About an hour later the balaclavas came back. Not our finest hour.'

'What d'you mean?'

Si shook his head. 'They said we were free. So we ran, didn't ask questions, just legged it.'

'The old guy said you cut a deal.'

'There was no deal! Except . . . except as it turned out, we were free but he wasn't. They let us go but kept Josh.'

'Did you know at the time?'

They looked at each other and eventually both nodded.

'As we were going through the door I looked back and there was Josh still sitting there,' Si said quietly, 'one of the balaclavas holding him in his seat. I'll never forget that look. Josh just stared back at me and then nodded slowly. I just left him. To whatever they're gonna do.'

Andy swore, Matt too. This was bad.

Thirteenth Bit

Rice plants on scree slopes

We discussed going back to the lock-up. I couldn't have found it, obviously, but the others figured they could. But no one was ready to cross that line. While we talked about rescuing him we felt brave. But the talking was enough, leaving the hostel was beyond us.

Miz pulled out her phone.

'I'm calling the police,' she said, 'and you two are going to tell them where he is.'

'He's not there, Miz,' I said. 'I told you, I was there and he's gone.'

'I don't care. We have to report this.'

Sal left at that moment and I went outside after her. We sat in silence on the steps. She was shaking a little.

'Tom, I want to go home,' she said, 'I'm scared. Really scared. I wish I wasn't but I don't understand what's going on. I want to be home, with my family. I feel lost here. Josh never promised this kind of thing. I don't want to abandon him, but . . . I can't do anything, anyway. Miz has got it under control. She'll tell the police about the lock-up and we can all leave.'

'They'll want statements.'

'Not from us. Let the others do that. You don't have to tell them you were there.'

I got up and paced. What to do, what to do?

'You don't have to say anything. Let Si and Jimmy sort it out. They're the action men, after all.'

'Well thanks for that vote of confidence.'

'Oh, come on, Tom. You know what you're like, you're more paranoid than me.'

Sirens wailed in another street. Time was running out. I kept pacing.

'I think I'm just like those rice plants on the scree slopes,' she said, sniffing and brushing tears from her eyes, 'Yea, that's me. I'm giving up because it's got tough.'

'You're not giving up, you're being sensible,' I said. 'He'd understand that.'

'So you'll come with me?' she pleaded, blasting me with those soulful eyes.

Two police cars turned into the road. I grabbed Sal's hand and we started up the street. I knew that if the cops confronted me I couldn't lie convincingly.

'Keep walking,' I said, and we did.

We went underground, bought tickets and couldn't sit still on the station. Sal kept pacing the platform, I kept twisting right and left, couldn't stop clocking the entrances. Every time I heard footsteps or a raised voice I was convinced they were after us. Whoever they were. There was still a delay on the line.

I overheard two Australians talking and the word was someone had fallen on the track. There was a terrible mess and a big investigation going on.

Eventually a train arrived. I dragged Sal on board and we collapsed onto an empty seat. We rode four trains, a bus and a taxi and spoke no more than two words to each other the whole journey. The taxi dropped us outside her house and I walked her to the door.

'I'm sorry about all this,' I said. 'Will you be all right?'

She nodded and, bizarrely, in that highly charged moment, on that incredibly stressed day, we kissed for the first time. I know that, in this day and age, that makes me sound emotionally retarded and the slowest guy on the planet, but that's just because I'm emotionally retarded and the slowest guy on the planet. No more clues. Our best mate was lost and abandoned, the guy who'd given me a life and brought Sal back from the dead. And there we were locking lips under the stars. Life's what happens while you're making plans.

News

I couldn't sleep. I tossed and turned. I walked on the seafront. I drank. Nothing would knock me out. I flipped on the TV at three in the morning and surfed for news.

Josh had disappeared. The summit was proving to be an incredible success without him. All the signs were good. The PM was pleased. The last thing I saw was a group shot of grinning politicians . . . then I woke up and it was 10.23 and 37 seconds. I knew that because the TV was still on and there was a clock in the corner just above Josh's left ear. Josh's left ear was swollen and a lot of blood had leaked from his right eye. There were a patchwork of bruises too but I think they'd disguised them with a deft airbrush. I hadn't expected to wake up to my mate's dead face. All I could do was stare at it and let the news permeate my brain. Apparently he'd been found on a piece of waste ground on top of a hill. Death had not been instantaneous. I stared and stared and

stared. It was a joke, wasn't it? A con-trick set up just to
see how we'd all react. No one really wanted Josh dead.
Too many people had been cheering for him in Truro. No
one hated him this much.

The phone rang. I knew it would be Sal.

'It's Jack. Where is everyone?'

'I thought they were still in the city.'

'Nope.'

'Where are you?' I asked him.

'Still in the city. At the hostel. Why aren't you?'

'I . . . ran away.' I told you I was a bad liar. 'I got
scared.'

'Did you see the news?'

'I did just now. I can't believe it, Jack.'

My voice suddenly broke and I couldn't quite believe
I was gonna break down on the phone talking to this
blond-haired cool dude. Then I realised he was saying
nothing on the other end.

'You OK, mate?'

He sniffed loudly. 'Not really,' he said and his voice
was slurred and thick and it struggled to make it down
the phone. 'It's been a nightmare.'

We both took a moment to breathe deeply for a while.

'You went back?' I asked.

'Yep,' he said and he cleared his throat. 'To the old guy in
the lock-up. I waited a long while before going in, though. I
plied him with money and whisky. He told me they had
taken Josh to some mansion in Kensington. Massive place.
They put him in the basement and beat him to a pulp, a
gang of them. Hung him upside-down and laid into him
with metal rods and electric cable. He never had a chance.
He was like something on a butcher's hook by the end.'

'No! How . . . Why? What the hell's going on?'

'It was a set-up, some thugs in bed with the government.'

'Government?' I couldn't believe it.

'Well, MI6, SAS, who knows? Some covert operation. They wanted him out of the way if he wouldn't co-operate.'

'But the beating . . .' My mind tore back to the sickening images in Tuol Sleng.

'They needed to make it look like some kind of gangland killing. Plus I think he insulted one or two high-ups along the way. I think a lot of those guys we saw sniffing around in suits and people carriers were government. They were terrified of him. They saw him as a loose cannon of the highest calibre, a maverick with supernatural power who could do anything.'

'How d'you know all this?'

'The old guy in the lock-up. Believe me, I can be persuasive, Tom.'

'How did it end?'

'Shot through the head. Apparently they have a soundproofed basement that's tiled from floor to ceiling. I guess it makes the clean-up that much easier afterwards.' He cleared his throat again. 'I'm coming home, Tom. Meet me tonight in the clearing, eh? Ten o'clock?'

The official story on Sky News was a highly creative piece of fiction. Worthy of the Man Booker Prize. Apparently Josh had a long list of alleged crimes to his name, including criminal damage, involvement in organised crime, disturbing the peace, inciting religious hatred, plagiarism and treason. Add to this the many rumours about his private life – drug and alcohol abuse, affairs with local women, sponging off society and not paying his taxes and it all made for a colourful obituary. His underlying aim was to destabilise the country. The evidence was detailed and convincing. He didn't have a hope. The world had obviously been delivered of an evil and callous individual. It was an open and shut case.

Murdered by the organised criminals he consorted with. His death was clearly a staged execution.

The only strange and comforting thought in all this was that it looked as if I wasn't the only one – all his friends had left him.

Sal cried. Of course she would. She's a healthy human being with no worries about looking stupid. So I eventually joined in. We sat in my flat on one armchair for the longest time and held each other. The sobs were so loud you couldn't hear the telly. When we calmed down I made beans on toast with two mugs of steaming tea. Comfort food. Then we went out and bought the day's papers. Later editions were running the story, in fact it was quite remarkable how much material they had been able to throw together in such a short time. *Panorama*, *Newsnight* and *Tonight* were also showing their own two-hour specials on Sunday night. *The Times* had a full colour supplement with photos and interviews. So much information in so little time.

Normality

We got a call from Miz. She and Si were still in London 'helping the police with their enquiries'. As far as they knew, the others had all done a runner. They were planning to come back in a day or two. Definitely by Tuesday. As Saturday began to die, Sal and I drove to the woods above the beach and walked for a while. There were a few families and dog-walkers ambling in the undergrowth, it was reassuring to see normality after so much madness. At ten o'clock, we slipped through the fence and into the clearing. A single figure was waiting in the dark. Hunched on a tree stump, a can of beer in one hand.

'Hi, Jack.'

'It certainly has been . . .' his speech was slurred, 'a bleeding hijack. You know, I hated that joke at school . . . Everywhere you went people said it to ya . . . and laughed as if it were the first time since the Big Bang . . .'

'You're drunk,' Sal said.

'Well, pardon me!' he said melodramatically, as Sal tried to grab his can.

For a moment they tussled in the dark. Beer slopped in the dry dirt in a circle round them. Sal was strong but Jack wasn't giving up his anaesthetic.

'Oh, keep it, then,' she said in the end. 'You blokes are all the same, bit of pain and you run and hide.'

'Run and hide? Run and hide! That's good coming from you.' Jack stood and stabbed a swaying finger at her. 'It wasn't me that buggered off out of London leaving him to die. It wasn't me that caught the first train home.'

Sal gave him a grim smile. 'No, and it wasn't us who walked out on him and left him in a dark lock-up with a bunch of killers,' she said.

'That's unfair. It was all confused. And anyway, I went back.'

'Later! When it was all safe.'

'Grief! Listen to you! You ran at the first sign of trouble. At least I tried to do something.'

Sal and Jack stared each other out from their respective corners. I held a hand up and stepped between them.

'Look, we all blew it,' I said.

'Oh well, that's all right, then.' Jack fell back onto his stump and poured an awful lot of his can down his throat.

'I don't suppose you've got one of those for us?' Sal asked.

Jack kicked at a carrier bag near his feet.

'Dive in,' he said, so we did.

We pulled up a couple of other tree bits and crouched near him, but not too near.

'D'you hear from the others yet?' he asked.

'Miz and Si are stuck in London,' Sal said. 'Back next week, they hope.'

'What are you gonna do?' I asked him.

He shrugged. 'Drink a lot and then go back to work. Forget it all happened. Start again. Don't know what I was thinking anyway. This summer's been like putting off the inevitable. I'm not cut out for this kind of life. Whatever this kind of life is. What about you?'

I glanced at Sal but she was looking at Jack.

'No idea. Drift aimlessly through the rest of my life probably,' I said.

A trashed painting

We tried calling the others but every single phone was switched off. Even Si's and Miz's. Everyone had gone to ground. Jack and Sal came back to mine and we sat around staring at Sky News till the small hours. It was like watching a bad B movie. They'd created Josh in their own image. New Age guru slaughtered following reports of corruption, manipulation and sleaze. People we'd never seen came on screen and gave in-depth accounts of fake miracles and abuse of power. The contradictions seemed to pass them by. If his power was fake, surely it would be hard to abuse it. A couple of famous authors appeared in the studio claiming he'd breached copyright and pinched their storylines. It was pitiful really.

At some point we fell asleep and I found myself on the beach. The sky was like a badly bruised face and there was a storm in the air. I felt a hand on my shoulder. I turned and started when I saw Jude.

He had blood all over his hands and a FedEx parcel under his arm. He pulled it out and handed it to me. His fingers left red gashes across the packet.

'I don't need this now,' he said.

'Are you OK?' I asked him but he shook his head.

His coat was spattered in blood and his eyes looked like pieces of rotting fruit.

'I went too far,' he said. 'I just wanted to change the world. Make it better. That's not a bad thing, is it?'

I shook my head. He pushed his hands in his pockets and pulled out thousands of pounds in used notes. Then I noticed that he had money everywhere, falling out of his pockets, dropping from his cuffs, stuffed inside his shirt . . .

'D'you think he can bring me back from the dead?' he said.

And the phone rang. It woke me so suddenly it gave me an instant headache. I glanced at the time on the TV. It was 4 a.m.

'It's Jude.'

'Jude! I was just dreaming about you. Where are you?'

'I'm back. I'm in the clearing. I've just driven back from London with Miz. I have something you have to see. Come now. I don't have much time, Tom. Come straight away. OK?'

I folded the phone and looked at the others. Jack stirred but rolled back over. Sal was out like a light.

I pulled on my jacket and slipped out the door. The streets were empty under a blood-red sky; no one would witness a bleary-eyed figure lurching through the town at daybreak. I started to run. The way into the clearing was as well concealed as ever. I pulled back the rhododendron bush, lifted the plasterboard and slipped through the break in the fence. There was a deafening crash as the wood fell back into place. The clearing was shrouded in darkness. The sun was coming up but there were so many trees lurching overhead the light couldn't get through. There was no sign of Jude but the clearing wasn't empty. Right in the centre there was an ominous dark mound. I moved closer. A bird flapped and screamed and smashed through leaves over my head. Somewhere in the undergrowth an animal was scratching around. I peered into the gloom and did my best to keep my nerves in check.

'Jude?'

Nothing. I spun round in a circle. Where was he? There was a rustle in the trees, an owl hooted overhead, and I saw a face in the bushes.

'Jude? Miz?'

I pushed the branches apart. The face disappeared. It was nothing more than a leafy shape fluttering in the breeze.

I turned back and went on into the clearing. I heard a noise and for a moment I was sure I heard breathing and saw the black mound move, I went closer and called out but there was no response. It was just a pile of clothes. A discarded bag full of dumped hand-me-downs.

No it wasn't.

It was . . .

It was a body bag. And it wasn't empty.

It was him. Josh. Somehow Jude had retrieved his body and brought it back here.

I knelt in the dirt and ran my hand along the contours of the corpse wrapped inside. Josh, dead. Cold and decomposing right here under my hands. I had to be sure so I reached for the zip. My fingers shook a little as I knelt by the head and clawed at the metal. Suddenly there was a disturbance above and a cone fell and thumped the ground beside me. I started, stood, looked up, swallowed hard and knelt down again. 'It's just the wind, it's just the wind, it's just the . . .' The zip was stuck, my fingers wouldn't work properly, the bag was old, the runners rusty. Everything was against me but I needed to see, I needed to know it was really all over. I pulled hard. It wouldn't budge. Harder. It started to move. One of my nails splintered as my finger slipped off the catch. I took hold again. It was loosening now. One good tug and I'd have it open. I steeled myself and yanked hard, falling backwards with the force. The teeth of the zip shot apart and yawned open. I scrambled forward to pull back the canvas folds, hesitating to brace myself for the sight of the damage to his face. I pulled, the bag fell open and I stared, my jaw dropping like a stone. There was the body all right. Face twisted away from me, blood smeared down the exposed cheek. I reached inside and grabbed the jaw and pulled. The flesh felt hard and cold, like chilled cardboard. There was caked blood everywhere. I twisted the body and studied the face. It was a mess, a terrible mess. But I still recognised him. I stared for a long time. A very long time. It wasn't Josh at all. It was Jude. He was here, dead. His face mangled like a trashed painting.

Mind's eye

The phone rang. I sat up. The headache hit me again, only this time it was real. I looked around. I was back in the flat. The TV was on and it was 7.50 a.m. Jack and Sal stirred.

'Hurry up and get that!' Jack mumbled.

I reached for my mobile.

'Tom, it's me, Miz. I'm with Jo, we hired a car and we're driving back. We'll be with you in an hour.'

'Do you have any news?'

'I'll show you when I see you.'

Show us? What did that mean? The others were awake too now. So we made tea and we waited. Jack and I paced the little yard below the back of my flat, nursing our mugs like they were winning lottery tickets. The birds were singing as if everything was fine. I didn't have the energy to shut them up.

'D'you think we'd have been drinking tea together in my garden if we'd never met him?' I said.

Jack shook his head. 'I wouldn't be with half you guys if I'd never met him. Maybe that was his mistake, putting together people who don't belong in the same room.'

'Why'd he do that?'

Jack shrugged. 'Manpower shortage, probably.'

Sal joined us. She was shivering so I pulled off my jumper and gave it to her. Then I shivered instead.

'Remember that prayer he told us,' she said.

Jack groaned. 'I'm not going all religious just cause things are falling apart,' he said. And he went in.

I muttered something about remembering it.

'Pray it with me, will ya?' she said.

'Really?'

'It's comfort, isn't it?'

So she prayed and I tried to keep up. In my mind's eye I could see him again, sitting on a mountain bike on the seafront. One of those cloudless days in the summer when we were sitting around swapping stories and smoking.

'Whatever you do don't pretend or put on funny voices when you talk to God. Everyone does it. Well, don't. For goodness' sake, he knows you inside out, he knows what you're really thinking. Say it like it is. And do it on your own, peer pressure's a terrible thing. Go for a walk or find a quiet corner.

*Don't try and be eloquent or preach sermons to other people.
Just talk. Say what's on your mind. Kneel and whisper if you
want or go to a cliff top and shout. Just stay in touch. Believe
it or not, he misses you when you break contact. If you need
some guidance then try starting with some lines like this –
God, you're a good father, we've seen bad ones, but you're a
good one. You're different and we want to give you respect.
Help us to see your kingdom and bring it down here to the
streets of this world. Please provide what we need each day,
and forgive us when we damage others, as we forgive the people who have damaged us. Steer us away from the things that
rob us of life, and when we get into danger – please show us a
way out . . .'*

We finished the prayer and Sal pressed against me
and we listened to the sounds of the day getting started.

*'Forgive us when we damage others, as we forgive the peo-
ple who have damaged us.'*

His words echoed around my head.

'D'you think he forgave them?' I asked.

'What?'

'He said forgive others – d'you think he forgave the
guys who beat him? And the politicians who authorised
it? And the people who paid for it? And Jude who
kicked it all off . . .'

I shivered as I suddenly remembered the dreams.

'When I died,' Sal said, 'I wasn't scared. It was as if I
was above myself and I could see everyone round the
bed and myself all cold and white. I saw you and Josh
and my dad burst in, and I could see my mum screaming and trying to pull Josh away. Then I heard this voice,
it was familiar and friendly and I looked over and saw a
shining figure waving me over. So I followed him, or it,
or her or whatever, and the room below faded away; my
parents, you guys, my life . . . it all went and instead
there was just mist everywhere. Then it cleared and I

was standing at these massive gates.' She laughed. 'So many jokes about those pearly gates . . . Well, I saw them. They just opened, I went in and it was amazing. Like a living portrait, a massive screen of greens and blues everywhere and I could hear the sounds of wildlife and people, music and conversation. People were alive, I mean really alive, laughing, talking, playing sport, building things, eating, dancing . . . I could taste this intensely sweet, clean air, and I could smell a familiar scent that I couldn't place, but it made me feel at home. And there were a million different colours, a thousand hues and shades I'd never seen in my life before.' She stopped and stared at the pale grey sky.

'Why d'you stop?' I asked.

'Well . . .' She looked at me. 'I heard his voice. Josh's voice. And it was annoying, it was like he was telling me off. Ordering me to wake up, and it was so unfair. I had to leave everything there and come back here.' She looked up again. 'Maybe Josh is up there now. What d'you think?'

'I don't want to think, I've thought too much lately.'

Fourteenth Bit

The murdered guru's battered corpse

We went in and immediately there was a rap at the door.
We looked at each other. The letterbox flipped up and a
voice hissed through it.

'Come on. Let us in!'

I opened the door a little and Jo and Miz pushed past
me and came inside. Their hands were shaking and their
breathing was unsteady.

'Have you seen Si?' Miz asked. 'Is he here?'

'We thought he was with you,' said Sal.

'No, he said he was going to look for Nat – he got
picked up again by the police. But listen, listen . . .'

'Do you want something to eat?' Sal asked. 'I'll get
you some breakfast.'

'Listen!' Jo said, but Sal wasn't listening.

'Sit down,' Miz said and she pushed Jack and me onto
the sofa. 'We've heard things.'

'What?' asked Sal.

'They've lost the body.'

Jack leapt up again. 'What?' he said.

'We went with Si back to see the old guy in the lock-
up. He was pretty out of it but he said they've lost the
body.'

'He was drunk!' said Jack. 'He lives on whisky and mouldy sandwiches.'

'Maybe, but look at this, we picked up this first edition on the way out of London.' She flung a newspaper at Jack. 'Front page, tiny box at the bottom there.'

'Revolutionary new breakthrough in invisible hearing aids?'

She rolled her eyes. 'Next to it.'

> ### Dead New Age Guru goes walkabout
> *The plot thickened overnight as news broke of the disappearance of Josh Churchill's body. The murdered guru's battered corpse had been placed in a Kensington mortuary overnight, police reported. Security guards had been posted. In spite of this, when police came to collect the body early this morning it was missing. It is rumoured that members of his illegal sect may have broken into the building. More to follow.*

'Illegal sect?' Sal said. 'Since when were we a sect?'

'Since when were we illegal?' I said.

'See if they're running the story on the TV yet,' said Miz.

Sal began flicking channels.

Jack began flicking through the paper.

'Oh my . . . have you seen this?'

'What?'

'Page 4. It's Jude.'

'What about him?' I said.

'He's dead. Listen, "Underground trains were severely disrupted on Friday when a 25-year-old man threw himself onto the line." It's Jude! Look at the picture.'

'Not more killing!' I yelled. 'This is . . .'

'No. They say it was suicide.'

'Sure, and they say Josh was a womanising New Age guru with links to the underworld. Yea, right!' said Miz.

'Jude was pretty down the last time I saw him,' I said.

Very down if you count the scene in my dream.

Jack's phone sang an old Bowie song, but he cut it off two bars in. 'Yea?' He listened for a while. 'It's Si,' Jack said to us. 'Sounds like he's on the motorway. Si, did you find Nat?'

I went close to listen to the conversation.

'Yep,' Si was saying, 'the Bill let him go. Who d'you think's driving?'

'Nat can't drive,' said Jack. 'He hasn't passed his test yet.'

'Ah,' replied Si. 'Well, we were in a bit of a hurry.'

'You're not in danger, are you?' I said.

'No, far from it. We'll tell you soon.' And Si hung up.

'Would you believe it,' I said. 'A traffic warden and he can't drive. That's Nat all over.'

We sat in front of *Sky News* the rest of the morning. The official line had us all in the dock. Dangerous punks who'd overpowered six security guys and carried off the corpse. We started to wonder whether we'd get a knock at the door pretty soon.

Around eleven, someone at News Inc. put two and two together over Jude and suddenly his death on the railway was all over the screen. He'd left an awful lot of blood on those tracks. When we did hear a knock on wood it wasn't the law, it was Andy, Matt and Jimmy; they all came in with their tails between their legs. No one knew what to make of the bodysnatching incident.

By three, we were all starving and tired of shouting insults at the telly. There was still no sign of Si and Nat.

'I'm going to get some takeout,' I said. 'Chinese OK? Sal?'

She shook her head. 'I'm not hungry,' she said.

'We have to eat something,' said Jo.

'I'll have Indian,' said Jimmy, raising a finger.

'Indian's another two streets away.'

'Then you'd better get going, hadn't you,' said Jimmy.

'There isn't an Italian, is there?' said Matt. 'I could murder pasta.'

'D'you have to put it like that?' said Jimmy.

'Like what?'

'Like – murder! You doghead!'

'Hey! Hey! Let's just get food,' I said. 'There's been enough violence lately. I'll get a whole selection and if you eat any it's up to you. But I've gotta get out of here, I'm going stir crazy.'

'How can you think about food now?' said Miz.

'Because life goes on – you have to pick yourself up and keep going, Miz. I've been here before, he's not the first person to die in my life. I don't wanna sit around staring at the walls and thinking about death.'

'I don't want to do that either.'

'Well, don't have a go at me for wanting some distraction from this madness.'

'Ease off, Tom,' said Jack. 'We're all wired right now.'

'Well, just back off, OK? I'm offering to do a good thing here. I'm not going to hide like some frightened kid.'

I clattered down the stairs and left 'em to it.

Space

It was quiet out there. But it was good to be away from the rumours and hearsay. I took a detour via the seafront and stood for a while staring out to sea, the wind ripping at my face. It occurred to me I hadn't offered to bring Sal. She may have appreciated this kind of space right now. I ambled cautiously towards the Indian, breathing deeply as I went. In the flat where the TV was full of sensation and prejudice, the walls had started to close in. Out here, where everything was normal, I was able to claim back some perspective. I had some banter with the guy at the takeaway. He'd got the story on in the background but was taking not a jot of interest in it. It was heartening to see such a careless attitude towards the media. In the Chinese it was even better, they were showing UK Gold and an episode of *Top Gear*. Now, that was good therapy. I sat there watching the lads messing about with cars and let it pull my brain away from the carnage for a while. I felt like I did the day we visited Tuol Sleng – I needed to see real life going on again so I could forget the hell for a while.

When I finally started limping home I was carrying four bags and too many cans of beer. Then I spotted the open door. The hallway into my flat was exposed to the world. The worst had happened. The police were there and we were all in trouble. I dropped three of the bags and ran. Down the path and up the stairs to my door. I could hear voices coming from inside, raised voices. They were yelling and shouting. Sal sounded very unhappy. I barged in and stood there, can of beer in one hand, a bag of bhajis in the other.

Everyone shut up and looked at me. There were no blue uniforms in sight. It was just the guys, standing around all yakking.

'Where's the fire?' Jimmy said, seeing me standing there like a cobra poised for the kill.

'I heard yelling. The door was open. I thought the Bill was here.'

And they started to laugh. That's when I noticed Si and Nat were back, cause they had the loudest laughs.

'Are you lot mental?' I shouted. 'Keep the noise down.'

Nat walked up to me, pressed his hands on my cheeks and stuck his face in mine. For one terrible moment I thought he was gonna kiss me.

'You missed him, dude!' he announced triumphantly.

'Missed who?'

I looked at Sal; surely she'd be an ally. But she was grinning stupidly too.

'He was here, Tom,' she said, quietly.

'Who?'

'Who d'you think?' boomed Si. 'Josh!'

And suddenly everyone was saying his name, like I'd never heard it before. I retreated under the onslaught and backed out onto the fire escape. Through the window I could see them all congratulating each other about something. Making me look a prat, probably. Sal slipped out and took me down into the yard.

'I'm sorry, Tom, I know it's unfair. We're just all so high.'

'On what?'

'The news. Didn't you hear? He's back!'

I stepped away and looked at her. Then slowly I shook my head.

'Tom,' she warned, 'don't start that. This isn't some news story now – your mates are all in there and everyone of them'll back me up. Josh isn't dead. He was here. Alive. Nat and Si had literally just got back and knocked at the front door when we heard a footstep on the fire escape out the back, and there he was. Si was well miffed because he wanted to break the news himself. They met him in London, Tom.'

I kept shaking my head. 'If you want to believe that – fine,' I said, 'it's a free country. But I'm not falling for it. Listen to yourself. You're dreaming. You're mad! He's in a ditch somewhere decomposing, or at the bottom of the canal with a ton of concrete in his pockets. Wake up, Sal.

This is bonkers. You heard what happened, you saw the pictures. He's dead. People don't come back from that. They really don't.'

'I did.' She said it so quietly, her sweet pleading eyes begging me to soften up. 'I did.'

I shook my head. 'You're deluding yourself. It's wishful thinking. You want it to be true but it isn't. It can't be. He's gone.'

'He was right there, Tom, speaking to us. We all heard him.'

'Well, he's gotta come right up to me and let me see daylight through the bullet hole in his temple before I'll swallow it. I swear if he's alive . . . then . . . it's . . . some sort of scam. I just . . . can't believe it.'

I don't know what got into me. (Aside from the obvious fact that only little boys in movies see dead people on a Sunday afternoon). I guess it must have been the shock of coming back to this fiasco. I was embarrassed to find myself the odd one out – everybody against me yet again. I was also annoyed about everybody else having a fine old time while I was out risking my life to get their prawn crackers and poppadoms. And most important of all I was bloomin' furious that I'd just wasted good money on food and beer for my so-called friends which I'd then chucked all over the street.

'Your lunch is on the pavement outside,' I said, and I pushed past her and out of the back gate.

I didn't know where I was going. I had no allies. I really was on my own this time; even Sal was in on the conspiracy.

The clearing seemed the best bet.

I smashed it up, but to be honest, it was just about the safest place to trash if you had to trash anywhere, there was so little damage to be done. I hurled handfuls of spent gun cartridges at the heavens but they all bounced back down to earth, many of them on me; I booted repeatedly and savagely at the rampant rhododendron bushes but they never gave in and always came back for more; so I thumped a lot of palm trees and nearly broke my hand. It all made very little impression. The only thing that changed was that I got worn out and eventually fell on my back in the centre of the clearing, in just the spot where I'd come across Jude's body bag. I lay there for a long time watching the clouds chase each other across the sky; the scene was soothing and I remembered Josh's last words to me: 'It's OK,' he said, 'I understand. Let go of Mike. Be yourself. One day at a time. You can do it.'

For the first time in my life, I became proactive. Two days later, with my courage screwed up in the pit of my stomach, I went to see my mum and dad and told them, as gently as possible, that I was finally getting over Mike's death. They may not have been, but I was.

My dad was quiet, his face strangely creased, but Mum and I talked a lot. And about subjects we'd never broached before. Not everything got solved, especially with Dad, but I felt I'd made some peace about it all, if only with myself. I went to see Sal, too.

'Let's get married,' I said. 'Let's get it together and move away and forget all this.'

Her face went from amusement to shock in the time it took to say those last fourteen words.

'Let's . . . wait,' she said guardedly. 'Believe me that's not a no, Tom. It's really not a no. But I have a hunch this isn't over yet.'

'I'm not going to change my mind,' I said.

'About which – the marriage or the resurrection?'

'Neither. Both.'

She smiled. We waited. A week went by.

I didn't see much of the others. I didn't need to; I still had their derisive laughter ringing in my ears. Andy came round a couple of times, Jack invited me over for poker and Nat made me go shooting. But that was it. That was as far as it went. It was them and me.

'Wanna see some daylight?'

Then Monday came round.

Si got together with Jack and they called a meet-up at Breakers. We'd been avoiding the Greyhound for fear of local attention. The allegations of bodysnatching were still rife in the news so we figured home ground was safest. Everyone was there and we were just about to get underway in the back room when there was a tap on the rear door. Jimmy sprung the fire exit bar and pushed it open, but there was no one there.

'Trouble?' asked Jack, but Jimmy shrugged.

'Nothing,' he said, so we carried on. Jimmy slammed the door shut.

'We all need to think hard about what we're going to do,' Si said. 'We're in limbo. Anyone got any ideas?'

'Let's ask Josh,' Matt said.

I snorted. 'Yea, right,' I said.

'Shut up, Tom.'

There was another knock on the door, louder this time.

'Oh, for . . .'

Jimmy bashed the bar and the door flew back. Still no one there.

'Leave it open,' said Jack.

'The problem for us,' said Jimmy, 'is that this is Mum's business and we have to decide if we're gonna stay.'

'Where is there to go?' I asked.

'Tom!' The voice came from outside, beyond the open fire door.

We gathered in a group and peered out into the early evening light. There was no one there.

'Tom!'

The voice was suddenly behind us, inside the room. I spun round. In that moment everything froze. Could have been a second, could have been a fortnight. He was there, grinning at me, wagging a finger in my direction.

'Watch this,' he said and he turned side on. 'Wanna see some daylight?' And he pointed to the indent in his temple. 'Come on, don't bottle out on me now.'

I shuffled towards him, regretting every word I'd said. He grabbed my collar and pulled me close. There was a bullet hole all right, but I couldn't tell you whether there was daylight, I'd seen enough.

'Josh!' I whispered and he gave me a bear hug.

I pulled away and crumpled onto a chair.

I muttered words that were between me and him. Some of the others overheard.

He helped me back up.

'Tom! You got what you wanted. I'm here. You're lucky. Plenty of people will have to trust without this kind of one-to-one.' Then he looked at the others and grinned again. 'I can walk through walls now you know,' he said and he winked.

Was he kidding?

He stayed around for a while and we bantered a lot. We all had massive questions but didn't ask them. Life, the universe and everything could wait. We had our mate back from the dead.

Later he slipped away and left us still talking – it was like that from then on. He'd come and go, and always be like the old Josh, but it wasn't the same. He picked his moments and then he'd be gone, and we never knew where he went. Often other people would tell us they'd bumped into him somewhere and we'd had no idea about it. He wasn't ours any more, I guess. He was on wide release now.

The old routine

We were sitting around playing poker, Si, Nat, Andy, Jack, Jimmy, Matt and me. Ten o'clock in the morning, believe it or not. It was a weird phase, like everything was great cause Josh was back, but there was nothing to fight for; he spent his time visiting old friends and having quiet chats with them. We began to revert back to the old ways. And poker at Jack and Jimmy's surf shack was one of the old ways. The old spark wasn't there, though; we wanted it to be like it was, but too much had happened to all of us. The most competitive thing these days was who could do the best shuffle. The guys went to elaborate lengths to prove themselves. Then Si chucked down his cards.

'I'm fed up of this. I can't sit around losing money, I got cars I should be fixing.' He stood, pushing his chair back so hard it toppled over. He didn't pick it up. He seemed at war with himself about something.

For some reason we all followed him. Jack and Jimmy didn't even tidy up the cards.

'We've got to get Keats' Merc sorted,' Si said when we got to the garage. 'He'll be sending the boys round.'

'Oh no, not Wallace and Gromit . . .'

'Shut up, just go into the office and stay out of trouble. And don't eat our Wagon Wheels.'

Andy stayed to help his brother, while the rest of us retired to the office to loll about on their desks, drink their coffee and eat their Wagon Wheels.

Five minutes later, Andy was bending over the bonnet and Si was under the car on a trolley. They couldn't see the new customer as he strolled in from the forecourt.

'How's business?'

'Brisk,' said Andy, still tinkering with the battery.

'And this one?'

Andy sighed. 'Give us time, we're getting there.'

'It'll be fine!' Si roared from under the chassis. 'Is that you, Keats?'

The guy began to drum his fingers on the wing.

Si heard and let out a thunderous roar.

'We're busy!' he said.

I slipped out of the office and helped myself to a Coke from their machine just then, and as I glanced up I spotted the figure in the cracked mirror on the wall above my head. He leant over the open bonnet, stuck his head deep inside for a minute, then reappeared covered in engine oil.

'Try it now,' he said.

Andy pulled his head out and looked.

Si snorted under the car.

'Leave the work to us,' he retorted.

'Try the engine.'

There was a dull silence then I heard Si react and bash his head on the chassis. He came out cussing and swearing; there was something very familiar about all this.

The stranger was now nowhere to be seen. He had wandered back out onto the forecourt.

'Try that engine!' Si barked, so Andy did.

It fired up first time and purred like a dream.

'Josh!' Si shouted, and he stumbled out of the garage.

We sat in the office and shared out the rest of the coffee. Josh had brought doughnuts so we tore them and passed them round.

'Fancy a stroll on the beach?' he asked, and we each shrugged in a non-committal manner, so he took that as a 'yes' and we went.

He spent a lot of time walking with Si, Jack not far behind. They clearly had some business to sort out and we weren't going to get in the way. So we let it happen.

As we passed Breakers, Si and Jack peeled off and went inside.

I found myself catching up with Josh.

'You doing OK, Tom?' he asked.

I told him about my trip to see my old mum and dad.

'Nothing can bring Mike back,' he said. 'Not even you impersonating him. You did the right thing.'

'Things are getting better,' I muttered. 'Like you said, Sal's helping me.' I kicked a nearby can. 'We're getting hitched.'

He couldn't suppress his reaction. I guess he didn't want to. 'Good man,' he said, smacking me on the arm. 'I take back all I said about ya!' Then he stopped. 'I know you don't like danger, Tom. I know you preferred staying in the dark, in a drunken stupor. It's an instinct to run and hide.'

My stomach was churning now. This wasn't supposed to be happening.

'Why . . . why are you talking about danger?' I said. 'What's that about?'

'Don't panic, Tom. A lot of good things will come your way.'

'I don't like the sound of that, it's like I have no choice.'

'Oh, you'll have a choice, Tom; you'll always have a choice. No one's taking away your mental ability or your personality. All I'm saying is the day may come when your faith is more important to you than your life.'

I laughed. 'I don't have much faith,' I said.

'Oh, you do. You may go down in history for something else, but it'll be your faith that etches you in the annals of time.'

'You've lost me now,' I said.

He put a hand on my shoulder. 'Pretty soon, Tom, I'm gonna walk up that hill,' he pointed to the far end of the beach where the cliffs cut sharply upwards towards the skies, 'and I won't come down again. Not for a long time. Chapter one'll be over. But don't panic, it's not the end of the book, this story's full of chapters, it'll run and run and run. Don't be in a hurry to begin chapter two, though; wait – for the energy and the inspiration.' He glanced back along the beach; we looked a motley crew. 'For now, pursue Sal with all your energy. Don't let her get away. She's amazing, she's beautiful, she's unique, and hopefully she may just keep you out of a life of crime.'

Fifteenth Bit

A life of contradiction

What was that thing he said? The summer's a natural aphrodisiac. You only have to walk outside your door and you're assaulted by meagre clothes and abundant flesh. Body parts everywhere. It just ain't fair. Now, ordinarily I'd welcome that kind of intrusion, but I was trying to go cold turkey, give up the old Sky Scandinavian Three, and in that kind of climate it was a nightmare.

And so I found myself in a newsagent's, my eyes pulling me towards the Men's Interest section. Apparently we blokes are interested in just two things, angling and naked women. I stared at the covers for a long time (the women, not the angling), my pulse racing. The shop was quiet, the girl behind the counter engrossed in her own magazine. I reached out, took a copy, and flipped the pages. I could sense my breathing speeding up. Then I heard a voice.

'Hi, Tom.'

I froze. It was Josh, I knew his voice. Could he see the material in my hands, the hungry look in my eyes? How long had he been there?

'Hi, Josh,' I said, still staring at the display of pink flesh, feeling like a humiliated schoolboy.

I braced myself, turned and held my hands up, the magazine still perched in my fist.

'You got me,' I said. 'Better shoot to kill.'

He frowned. 'Don't know what you're on about. Come on, let's get pancakes. I need a chat with you.'

And before I knew it, the mag was back on the stand and we were walking down the street.

'I know you loved Cambodia, but there's another place you should think about.'

He handed me a map.

'I'm not sure I can do this, Josh. I'm . . . too wayward.'

He laughed. 'Wayward; kind of an old-fashioned word. Everyone's wayward, Tom. Everyone. Heroes, villains, saints, sinners. The good, the bad, the ugly. Everyone needs a ride home. You know, Tom, no one has the high moral ground in life. Any guy who ever looked at a woman and had sexual designs on her – that's the same as sleeping with her.'

I shook my head. 'Then I'm sunk.' And I handed the map back.

'Exactly.'

I didn't get it.

'Josh, I've been meaning to ask you – that wedding we went to, your cousin's, what happened? I heard something about free booze?'

He laughed. 'They ran out of wine, Tom, and things were about to get very embarrassing. My mum wanted me to fix it.'

'I never really understood what went on there . . .'

'When I was little, my mum was given this prediction about me, a prophecy about what I was gonna become, and ever since she'd been looking for a chance to let me shine. So when she saw the problem at the wedding she figured I could fix it. Thing was – I didn't want the publicity. You change 150 gallons of water into wine and every wedding planner for a thousand miles is gonna be knocking on your door. So in the end I did it quietly.'

'You turned 150 gallons of water into wine? How? How d'you do something like that?'

He grinned a little sheepishly. 'Same way you make burgers for a street full of people. Cautiously. People love miracles – you got to handle them with care.'

We came to the coffee shop and he pushed the door open for me.

'You say you're sunk, Tom,' he said as we grabbed a table. 'But what's so special about you? Everyone has their Achilles heel. Look around you, the girl over there, the sweet granny with her trolley, the two road sweepers out the window, the boy behind the counter. It's part of life. Everyone's weak and everyone's doomed. Except they're not. You may not believe this Tom, but I didn't have to stay in that lock-up. I didn't have to go through all that stuff. I chose to do it, to benefit others.'

'I don't get it.'

'There's more to this than can be grasped now. But think about this – wouldn't it be great to have some way of diffusing all the destructive elements in life? Some way of sucking the poison out?'

'But what's that got to do with what happened?'

'Look back in the past, Tom; history is littered with those who chose to make a sacrifice to benefit others.'

'But what did difference did it make? People still suffer, people still have terrible lives.'

'Yea, they do. The world is full of good news and bad – the two co-exist. The damaging stuff still goes on. The world's a hard place and there's plenty of trouble in it. The kingdom of good has come amongst the kingdom of bad. You know, people regularly feel remorseful about their crimes and misdemeanours, but it's the gift of God that one person has ultimately settled the debt. Swabbed the wound. For the people and the planet.'

'But the planet's getting worse.'

He nodded thoughtfully. 'But one day it'll all begin again. A new planet, a new start.'

He tapped his chest. 'The problem is this – to decide to put your faith in any of this is to choose a life of contradiction. Believe in something greater than yourself and you'll fall short of it. It's easier to despise it and bury your hope. But God understands what makes the world work best; don't overlook that. My advice to you, Tom, is grab life, get out there and do some living.' And he shoved the map back at me. 'I'm not asking you to do anything but be true to yourself. This is the job for you, mate. Now I'm gonna have the full monty here, eggs, bacon, pancakes – what about you?'

I didn't understand it. I'll tell you that now. I felt better for seeing him. But I understood less.

The day came

It arrived, that day he'd talked about, that day I was dreading. Once again I had no idea what was going on. Not at the time. Not a clue. He took us for a stroll on the beach. We were laughing and messing about as usual. Jimmy was kicking a ball about, Matt was listening to his iPod and occasionally blasting forth with his own version of the songs. 'Bohemian Rhapsody' sounded particularly bad. Jack and Miz were arm-in-arm, Sal and I a little more discreet. Nat had brought his mountain bike and was trying it out on the sand, attempting wheelies and kicking up gritty golden sprays. Si and Andy were trailing behind, unusually quiet. As if they knew what was coming.

'It's a good thing you brought that mountain bike,' Josh suddenly called out.

Nat didn't hear so I asked the question.

'Why?'

''Cause we're going up that mountain.'

And he pointed off in the distance, towards that hill, towards that place he'd promised would be the end of it all. And again I had that feeling, that *everything's falling apart* feeling in the pit of my stomach. Many things had caused it over the years and here it was again. I said nothing.

The others still chatted on as we walked up. Sal was telling me something about a distant cousin who refused to come to the wedding on account of the rumours about us. What rumours?

I dropped back and joined Si and Andy in the ranks of the silent. We started up the hill and, ironically, Nat left his bike at the bottom.

As we made the top and Josh turned to look at us, I started gabbling, anything to put off the moment.

'Jude talked about you changing things big time,' I said. 'You know, making a difference to everyone on the planet. You haven't done it yet, so you can't go. You've still got this last job to finish. Burgers for the world or whatever.'

He laughed. 'It's not about burgers for the world,' he said.

'But you could make poverty history, dude, and end global warming and destroy the drug cartels. You could, couldn't you? No more worst case scenario, right, dude?'

Josh looked at Nat; Nat's face was willing him to say yes.

'It doesn't work like that, Nat. Those things will end one day, but you have to wait, live with the bad alongside the good. I know that sounds like a cop-out, but there are other things to be done.'

We shook our heads. I think none of us got it at that point. If he had some jaw-dropping, sidewhacking power that could change things – why wouldn't he use it?

He turned and stared off into the distance. The sea was grey and the sky looked like there was a storm on offer.

'I'll miss this view,' he said.

'When did we ever come up here?' Jack asked.

'You didn't. I did. When I wanted to escape.' He studied our faces. 'Things'll go quiet for a while, but go back home and wait. This isn't the end.'

'Don't go . . .' It was Si. 'Don't do it, Josh. You don't have to. We were just getting going. Just getting the hang of it.'

Si's face showed the strain, he was battling to hold back a volcano inside.

'You'll get the hang of it, believe me. But that's why I've got to go. I can only be in one place at one time; you guys can go all over the world.'

'Come with us all over the world.'

He shook his head, paused and said, 'Actually, I will be with you all over the world.'

And we didn't get that either. Then he did the worst thing, he started to walk round our little circle of mates and he started to say goodbye. I hated that. I could hear little bits of his conversations with the guys and it all sounded so final. I could feel the emotion brewing in my chest. I didn't want this, I really didn't want this.

'Tom! Where you going?'

I looked back. I'd started on down the hill.

'I . . .' I swallowed the lump in my throat but it wouldn't go. 'I can't do this.'

He waved me back, then came towards me and met me halfway.

'Listen, Tom, I know it seems hard now; the last thing in the world I want to do is leave my friends . . .'

And that was it. I crumbled and started to sob like a big girl. He grabbed me and gave me a bear hug.

'It will be all right, Tom, grief's no bad thing, and you've had your fair share of it.'

And it came out then, all over his shirt, ruining his clothes. Eventually I straightened and looked at him. There were tears on his cheeks too and his face was flushed. He grinned and sniffed.

'I've loved knowing you, Tom. You've been a great mate. And we will see each other again.'

He hugged me once more and then he stepped away and I felt another set of arms pull me close. It was Sal, I knew that without opening my eyes. I didn't look up. I didn't want her to see me looking like this. It didn't occur to me that she was looking like this too.

'Remember what's been happening,' he said, and his voice became more distant, as he was walking away. 'All the stuff in London. Spread the word.'

And he went quiet. Everything went quiet. Then Jack spoke.

'How'd he do that?'

I looked up.

'How'd he do wha . . .'

He'd gone.

'Where is he?'

They were all looking up, mouths like the Channel Tunnel. But there was no sign of Josh. I spun and stared back down towards the beach. Nothing. Sal pointed up.

'He's up there, Tom,' she said in her usual quiet way.

I looked up. There was just a skulking grey cloud.

'What d'you mean, he's up there?'

'Blimey,' Si said, 'did you see that? I mean he just went . . . Va voom!'

And he laughed. For no reason. Then Jimmy laughed too. Why were they laughing?

What? What happened? What did I miss?

'What are you doing up here?'

I turned towards the strange voice.

There was a tall guy standing next to us, in a gleaming silver leather coat, a huge white husky straining on a lead next to him.

Jimmy's laughter stopped dead. 'None of your business, mate,' he said.

The husky let loose a sly growl but the tall guy jerked the leash and silenced it.

'Well, I'm sure he'll be back one day, but not now. You guys better get back down there and start the waiting.'

'Dude! You are totally out of order, man. What you talking about?'

Nat squared up to the stranger but Jack pulled him back. He ran a hand through his blond spikes.

'How d'you know about this?' Jack asked.

The tall guy smiled. 'Trust me. I know,' he said.

Pact with God

I guess that was about a month after the London stuff. We went back to our lives and kept meeting up and reminding each other of the things that had happened. I couldn't quite see the point myself, but Si kept calling meetings and if you didn't go he sent the boys round – namely Nat and Andy. Jack and Jimmy tried going to church for a couple of weeks, but it wasn't their thing so they soon dropped off. I really missed Josh. I mean, really. I kept spotting those moments when he should have turned up but didn't.

Sal and I went on with our plans for getting hitched. Three weeks went by. The news stories about Josh began to disappear. As far as the media were concerned it was ancient history now. Just that New Age guru – once flavour of the month, now dead and forgotten. They soon lost interest in the stories about a missing corpse. They couldn't get any exclusive pictures of Josh, he was keeping out of the limelight, and anyway there were other reputations to fry.

I remember the day very clearly. 'I Saved the World Today' was playing out of a first-floor window as I made my way to the clearing to meet the others. Sal was waiting on the corner by the front of the Old Mariner, and for some reason she was humming it too. She must have heard it as well. It was a bright September day, almost back to what the summer had been. We slipped through the fence and found the others in the clearing. Jack and Jimmy were playing poker with Nat and Andy. Si was checking his messages with one hand and strumming his beat-up old guitar with the other, Matt was flicking through songs on his iPod and hey, what d'ya know, ended up singing along tunelessly about the world and saving it; I couldn't get away from Annie Lennox. The woman's a prophet and doesn't know it. Miz turned up after us with Jo and a few others. There were a few guys I didn't know that well too, lads who'd started hanging around in the past few weeks. In the end there must have been twenty-five of us in that clearing.

'Big match on today,' said Jack. 'Argyle are coming down. The town'll be packed.'

'Oh, great. Let's go to Plymouth for the day,' said Matt.

'I'm going to the match, dudes,' said Nat. 'Got me some tickets!'

'Yes!' Jimmy punched the air and congratulated himself enthusiastically as he cleared a stack of chips from the centre of the poker circle.

Si stepped up. His face was serious. 'Let's be quiet for a bit,' he said.

'Why?'

'Well, let's remember Josh. I bought some doughnuts, I thought we could share 'em out and tell the new guys some of the old stories.'

'What? Again?' said Nat. 'I'm tired of just repeating the old stories. We should get some new ones.'

'What d'you mean?'

'Well . . . I wanna do something, not just talk . . . let's go back to Cambodia – that was a cool gig!'

'I've got an idea for a song,' Si said.

We all looked at him.

'What?' said Nat.

'You know, a song about Josh and the stuff we did with him.'

'He didn't tell us to sing songs.'

'No, but I'm fed up of this waiting . . .'

'I wanna hear it . . . the song . . . I wanna hear it.' It was Sal. I could have killed her.

There was a mixed bag of agreement and groaning, and for some reason the groaners lost out. People sat round in the dirt, leaning on each other and looking like something out of a Broadway musical while Si pulled an old notebook from his back pocket and thumbed through it.

'How many songs you got in there?' asked Jimmy.

'A few. Here we are.'

'Si, just one question, dude,' said Nat. 'You can't sing.'

'That's not a question, Nat, and I can actually.'

And he could. He wasn't Freddie Mercury but he wasn't Miss Piggy either. I forget the words now but it was something about the guy who hated oppression and loved justice and bigged up the humble and put down the proud and made you feel better about yourself, not worse. It was good. And later on they used to sing it a lot. I wasn't ever that much into the singing thing, but then I'm just generally miserable anyway.

The song is important because it was just as Si was into the second chorus that it happened. The sky suddenly darkened, like the weather was going to unleash a storm, then lights began to shine out of the trees at us. It was like something out of a Spielberg movie. I swear I thought it was a police raid. I honestly expected to hear dogs and sirens at any minute. I figured they'd finally decided to put us all away. We all swivelled and jumped up and stared into the undergrowth. The lights grew whiter and shone right into our faces so we couldn't see. Then the storm started closing in, the wind rattled through the trees and kicked around the clearing like it was trying to surround us. It was so violent that cans and cartridges were kicking up in the sand and battering our ankles. For a moment the sound was deafening and, with the light blinding our eyes, we lost all sense of perception. I flopped down onto the dirt and I felt Sal drop beside me. By this point I was convinced it was aliens, either that or Josh was staging some elaborate comeback. One way or another this was no ordinary Cornish sea storm. Then the noise began to die and the lights dimmed and when I looked around it was like everybody's head was lit up, like their hair was on fire. I started up to go and beat out a few flames but Sal pulled me back. She pressed her mouth to my ear.

'This is what he was talking about,' she whispered. 'Honest! I bet this is what he meant.'

What he meant when?

'He said – wait. Remember?'

I did then, vaguely. I'd been waiting so long I'd forgotten I was waiting.

Suddenly everything went away. The wind, the lights, the storming sky. Nothing left but daylight and silence. We blinked at each other and held our breaths. We may still have been there now if Si hadn't leaped up.

'I've got an idea,' he said. 'Come on.'

And he was up and off, crashing through the undergrowth as if he needed something desperately. We did our best to keep up.

Of course we hit the crowds once we got out onto the seafront, people milling everywhere, just like the day in Truro when Josh rode on the moped.

'We'll never get through this lot,' I called, trying to grab Si.

'I'm not trying to,' he shouted back and he jumped onto a nearby dustbin.

He sliced his fingers into the corners of his mouth and did the loudest wolf whistle in the world. Everything came to a stop, which was amazing because there was a lot of people and a lot of noise. Not only that but some of the others were on dustbins too – Jack, Jimmy, Miz, Jo, Andy and Matt. They were all dotted around in the crowd. And then there was a moment when nothing happened. It felt like a thousand years. Si stood there, turning a 360 on the bin. People looked up expectantly; maybe they thought it was a circus act or something. I think they expected juggling or tap-dancing. Then Si opened his mouth and I swear it was louder than I ever heard him speak before. Or since.

'Everybody, listen up! You're here for the match, yea? Good one! Well, before you go, I got something to tell you. Remember that New Age guru who got murdered at the Gore Summit? Well, we got good news. He didn't die! Well, he did die, but he didn't stay dead. And there's a reason. This time is a moment in history. And it's your moment if you want it. When Diana died, Elton John sang about her life being snuffed out like a candle in the wind and everybody cried and brought flowers, remember? Well, we tried to snuff out Josh's life like that. But we couldn't do it and we don't need any flowers for him. Everybody's looking for a hero, right? Everybody wants someone to save the planet and get us out of this mess we're in. Well, Josh is the guy. The guy we tried to kill is the one who can help us. Now it's up to you, you don't have to believe us. But we just want to say what Josh would say, come with us and try it. Take a walk and see where it leads you. You don't need lots of faith, you don't need to be religious and you certainly don't need to be good. You just need to start. Josh had a cousin who predicted this would happen. Well, here it is. We're going down on the beach right now, and if you wanna go to the match that's fine. But if you wanna take a risk we'll be down there and you can make a pact with God. Sealed with sea water. I'm done. Thanks for your time.'

As Si talked, and I don't know where he got all those words from, the others echoed them round the crowd. I swear I even heard snatches of Urdu and Spanish coming from a couple of the guys – which was odd cause none of us knew any other lingo. The sound travelled and there must have been hundreds of people listening by the end. From all over the place.

When he'd finished, Si jumped down and we followed him to the sea. I didn't dare look back, I couldn't face the thought that no one would come, or worse still, just two old codgers and a dog. When we reached the water and had nowhere else to go, Sal came and stood in front of me and pointed over my shoulder, willing me to turn.

'Look.'

I grimaced at her.

'Look!' She dug her fingers in my shoulder and pushed.

I turned.

I don't know how it happened, cause this wasn't Cambodia and we weren't Josh, but there they were. Hundreds of 'em. They'd all come down with us, and they were lining up along the beach, some of them already scooping up sea water and splashing their faces with it.

This wasn't just a new start for them. It was new for all of us.

Si struck up with his song again and a couple of kids grabbed old veggie oil drums and added rhythm. People were laughing and crying and shouting and dancing. I don't know if anyone really grasped what was going on. But we just went with it. It ran on till sundown, people coming up, telling us things, giving us stuff, getting us to say prayers for them and their kids. And we were exhausted when the last of them disappeared to their cars. I don't know who won the football that day, or if anyone was there to see it, but apologies to both teams.

As Sal and I wandered back up the sand, leaving dozens of teenagers sitting around singing and laughing, I heard it again – the Annie Lennox song. I think Josh was having a laugh. I think he kept reaching down and retuning the radios. Whatever, it seemed like a little bit of the world had been saved that day. And, for just a short time, the bad things left town.

Final Bit

As I sit here now, ten years on, staring up at that tiny cell window I see traces of light. Shafts of sun marking the end of another day. Maybe even my final day. And in the faint shadows on the floor I see an image of his face, and I hear him as if it were yesterday, standing on that seafront, looking me in the eyes and willing me to keep going. It was on a reckless, windy day and he was standing with his face into the full blast.

'You just need to break out of that old place you're in. Kick down the walls of that flimsy cardboard box. There's a bigger world out there, Tom. But you've gotta find it. Keep going, don't give up; keep asking, keep knocking on those doors. Never give up.'

Nat was there too, half-listening to The Killers on Matt's iPod and half-listening to Josh. Josh picked up Nat's bike and sat astride it, then carried on.

'The signs of God are everywhere – in the earthy, normal things of life. The trick is spotting them. Having the eyes and ears to see what's going on and what matters. People want to feel God, they want to look up at the skies and see something supernatural, something bigger. But if God made this natural stuff in the first place, why would he not use it as his weapon of choice? Why would he not use ordinary people, if that's what he created?

Maybe the most supernatural thing on the planet is ordinary life.'

Josh leant down and scooped some sand and let it run through his fingers before going on.

'God's been hijacked by the churches and the temples. They try to tell you he's in a box called religion. But he just broke out. He's walking the streets. He's playing football, he's on MTV. He's acting in the latest blockbuster, headlining at Glastonbury. He's under the bridge and over the motorway. He's all over the place. He snuck out of the buildings when no one was looking.'

'How do you know?' I said. 'I don't see him.'

'Yes you do, you just don't know you see him. If you want to find him, you can. You have to open your eyes, there are clues everywhere. But you have to look. Look for the signs and then work out what they mean.'

So I did, and look where it got me. Alone. Wounded. Poor. A stranger in a strange land. But I did find him, and now soon I'll see him again. Maybe even today. Do I regret anything? Of course. Plenty. It's been a tough old road, and I wanted to give up and go back to beer and porn many times. And sometimes I did. But Sal and the Boss kept me going. She *was* the Boss for me on many occasions. I miss Sal, dearly. They won't let all her letters through. But as far as I know she's back home putting all her energy into campaigning for my release. I don't regret choosing the life I chose. And I don't regret ending up in this prison because of it. I just miss her.

And all the others? Well, Andy ended up in Greece somewhere, Si upsticked his family and went to Italy, Jimmy didn't make it. He got into an argument over Josh one night and a gang laid into him. Some thug named Paul started it all. Jimmy never recovered from the beating. No one got charged. I heard bad things about Nat, too; they say he's in jail somewhere. Matt's in Saudi

Arabia. He's doing well and I heard that Jo went to America. Miz is doing what she always wanted to do – running the country, and the last thing I knew of Jack, he was writing a book, stuck out on some island somewhere.

Well, I guess that brings me to the end. I've just spent the last twenty minutes etching my epitaph into the cement floor. I have to do it quietly, cause you get a beating for doing anything but sitting still here. But you have to do something, so I've left my message to the world, and I'd say it to anyone: Choose life, because you don't have a lot of choice when it comes to death.

Thanks for reading.

Tom.

Further Reading

In the Fifth Bit, there are references to two books. If you'd like to read them, here are the details.

David Chandler, *Voices from S-21: Terror and History in Pol Pot's Secret Prison* (University of California Press, 2000). Loung Ung, *First They Killed My Father* (Edinburgh: Mainstream Publishing, 2001).